HOUSE OF EARTH

HOUSE of EARTH

A NOVEL

WOODY GUTHRIE

Edited and Introduced by
Douglas Brinkley and Johnny Depp

FOURTH ESTATE • *London*

infinitum
nihil

First published in Great Britain by
Fourth Estate
A Division of HarperCollins*Publishers*
77–85 Fulham Palace Road
London W6 8JB
www.4thestate.com

For more information about Woody Guthrie, please visit
www.woodyguthrie.org.

1 3 5 7 9 10 8 6 4 2

A catalogue record for this book is available from the British Library.

ISBN 978-0-00-750985-0

Designed by Leah Carlson-Stanisic

Typeset by Palimpsest Book Production Ltd, Falkirk, Stirlingshire
Printed in Great Britain by Clays Ltd, St Ives plc

TO

Nora Guthrie

AND

Tiffany Colannino

AND

Guy Logsdon

I ain't seen my family in twenty years
That ain't easy to understand
They may be dead by now
I lost track of them after they lost their land

—BOB DYLAN, *"Long and Wasted Years"*

And seeing the multitudes, he went up into a mountain:
and when he was set, his disciples came unto him:
And he opened his mouth, and taught them, saying,
Blessed are the poor in spirit: for theirs is the kingdom
of heaven.
Blessed are they that mourn: for they shall be
comforted.
Blessed are the meek: for they shall inherit the earth.

—MATTHEW 5:1–5 (*King James Version*)

CONTENTS

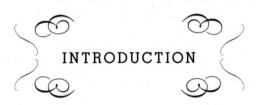

INTRODUCTION

*Life's pretty tough. . . . You're lucky if
you live through it.*

—WOODY GUTHRIE

1

On Sunday, April 14, 1935—Palm Sunday—the itinerant sign painter and folksinger Woody Guthrie thought the apocalypse was knockin' on the door of Pampa, Texas. An immense dust cloud—one that had emanated from the Dakotas—swept grimly across the Panhandle, like the Black Hills on wheels, blotting out sky and sun. As the dust storm approached the town, the bright afternoon was eclipsed by an ominous darkness. Fear engulfed the community. Had its doom arrived? No one in Pampa was safe from this beast. Huddled around a lone lightbulb in a shabby, makeshift wooden house with family and friends, Guthrie, a Christian believer, prayed for survival. The demented winds fingered their way through the loose-fitting windows, cracked walls, and wooden doors of the house. The people in Guthrie's tight quarters held wet rags over their mouths, desperate to keep the swirling dust from asphyxiating them. Breathing even shallowly and irregularly was an exercise in forbearance. Guthrie, eyes shut tight, face firm, kept coughing and spitting mud.

What Guthrie experienced in Pampa, a vortex in the Dust Bowl, he said, was like "the Red Sea closing in on the Israel children." According to Guthrie, for three hours that April afternoon a terrified Pampan couldn't see a "dime in his pocket, the shirt on your back, or the meal on your table, not a dadgum thing." When the dust storm finally passed, locals shoveled dirt from their front porches and swept basketfuls of debris from inside their houses. Guthrie, incessantly curious, tried to reconcile the joy of being alive with the widespread despair. He surveyed the damage in Pampa the way a veteran reporter would have done. The engines of the usually reliable G.M. motorcars and Fordson tractors had been ruined by thick grime. Huge dunes had accumulated in corrals and alongside wooden ranch homes. Most of the livestock had perished in the storm, the sand clogging their throats and noses. Even vultures hadn't survived the maelstrom. Images of human anguish were everywhere.

Some old people, hit the hardest, had suffered permanent damage to their eyes and lungs. "Dust pneumonia," as physicians called the many cases of debilitating respiratory illness, became an epidemic in the Texas Panhandle. Guthrie would later write a song about it.

To express his sympathy for the survivors of that Palm Sunday, Guthrie wrote a powerful lament, which set the tone and tenor of his career as a Dust Bowl balladeer:

> *On the fourteenth day of April,*
> *Of nineteen thirty-five,*
> *There struck the worst of dust storms*
> *That ever filled the sky.*
> *You could see that dust storm coming*
> *It looked so awful black,*
> *And through our little city,*
> *It left a dreadful track.*

In the spring of 1935, Pampa was not the only town that had been punished by the agony and losses of the four-year drought. Sudden dust cyclones—black, gray, brown, and red—had also ravaged the high, dry plains of Kansas, Nebraska, Oklahoma, Arkansas, Texas, Colorado, and New Mexico. Still, nothing had prepared the region's farmers, ranchers, day laborers, and boomers for the Palm Sunday when a huge black blob and dozens of other, smaller dust clouds quickly developed into one of the worst ecological disasters in history. Vegetation and wildlife were destroyed far and wide. By summer, the hot winds had sucked up millions of bushels of topsoil, and the continuing drought devastated agriculture in the lowlands. Poor tenant farmers became even poorer because their fields were barren. Throughout the Great Depression, the Great Plains underwent intolerable torment. The prolonged drought of the early 1930s had destroyed crops, eroded land, and caused many deaths. Thousands of tons of dark topsoil, mixed with red clay, had been blown down to Texas from the Dakotas and Nebraska, carried by winds of fifty to seventy miles per hour. A sense of hopelessness prevailed. But the indefatigable Guthrie, a documentarian at heart, decided that writing folk songs would be a heroic way to lift the sagging morale of the people.

Confronted with dreariness and absurdity, with poor folks in distress, many of them financially ruined by the Dust Bowl, Guthrie turned philosophical. There *had* to be a better way of living than in rickety wooden lean-tos that warped in the summer humidity, were vulnerable to termite infestation, lacked insulation in subzero winter weather, and blew away in a sandstorm or a snow blizzard. Guthrie realized that his neighbors needed three things to survive the Depression: food, water, and shelter. He decided to concern himself with the third in his only fully realized novel: the poignant *House of Earth*.

A central premise of *House of Earth*—first conceived in the late 1930s but not fully composed until 1947—is that "wood rots." At one point in Guthrie's narrative, there is a tirade against forestry products that rot down . . . sway . . . keel over. Someone curses at a wooden home: "Die! Fall! Rot!" Scarred by the dust storm of April 14, Guthrie, a socialist, damned Big Agriculture and capitalism for the degradation of the land. If there is an overall ethos in *House of Earth*, it's that those with power—especially Big Banks, Big Lumber, Big Agriculture—should be chastised as repugnant robber barons and rejected by wage earners. Woody was a union man. But his harangues against the powers that be are also tinged with self-doubt. Can one person really fight against wind, dust, and snow? Isn't venting one's spleen futile in the end?

Scholars who devote themselves to Woody Guthrie are continually amazed by how much unpublished work the Oklahoma troubadour left behind. He had an unerring instinct for social justice, and he was a veritable writing machine. During his fifty-five years of life, he wrote scores of journals, diaries, and letters. He often illustrated them with good-hearted cartoons, watercolor sketches, and comical stickers. Then there are the memoirs and his more than three thousand song lyrics. He regularly scribbled random ideas on newspapers and paper towels. And he was no slouch when it came to art. But *House of Earth*—in which wood is a metaphor for capitalist plunderers while adobe represents a socialist utopia where tenant farmers own land—is Guthrie's only accomplished novel. The book is a call to arms in the same vein as the best ballads in his Dust Bowl catalog.

The setting for *House of Earth* is the mostly treeless, arid

Caprock country of the Texas Panhandle near Pampa. This was Guthrie's hard-luck country. He was proud that the Great Plains were his ancestral home. It's perhaps surprising to realize that Guthrie of Oklahoma—who tramped from the redwoods of California to subtropical Florida throughout his storied career—first developed his distinctive writing style in the windswept Texas Panhandle. Guthrie's treasured Caprock escarpment forms a geological boundary between the High Plains to the east and the Lower Plains of West Texas. The soils in the region were dark brown to reddish-brown sand, sandy loams, and clay loams. They made for wonderful farming. But the lack of shelterbelts—except the Cross Timbers, a narrow band of blackjack and post oak running southward from Oklahoma to Central Texas between meridians 96 and 99—left crops vulnerable to the deadly winds. Soil erosion became a plague, owing to misuse of the land by Big Agriculture, an entity that Guthrie wickedly skewers in the novel.

Guthrie, it seems, knew more about the Caprock country than perhaps any other creative artist who ever lived. He knew the local slang and the idioms of the Panhandle region, the secret hideaways, and the best fishing holes. Throughout *House of Earth*, Guthrie uses speech patterns ("or something like that"; "shore cain't"; and "I wish't I could") with sure command. Exclamations such as "Whooooo" and "Lookkky!" help establish Guthrie's populist credibility. He had lived with people very similar to the novel's hardscrabble characters. His slang expressions are lures similar to those found in O. Henry's folksy short stories. Building on Will Rogers's large comedy repertoire, Guthrie, in a little pamphlet titled *$30 Wood Help*, gave a thumbnail impression of his beloved Lone Star State while carping about the lumber barons turned loan sharks. "Texas," he wrote, "is where you can see further, see less, walk further, eat less, hitch hike further and travel less, see more cows and less milk, more trees and less shade, more rivers and less water, and have more fun on less money than anywhere else."

House of Earth has a literary staying power that makes it more than just a curiosity: homespun authenticity, deep-seated purpose, and folk traditions are all apparent in these pages. Guthrie clearly knows the land and the marginalized people of the Lower Plains. In the novel, he draws portraits of four hard-luck characters all recognizable, or partly recognizable, to readers familiar with his songbook: the dutiful tenant farmer "Tike" Hamlin; his feisty pregnant wife, Ella May; a nameless inspector from the US Department of Agriculture (USDA) who asks farmers to slaughter their livestock to raise farm prices; and Blanche, a registered nurse. When Tike, full of discord, lashes out at his own ramshackle house—"Die! Fall! Rot!"—he is speaking for all of the world's poor living in squalor. Like all of Guthrie's work, which is often erroneously pigeonholed as mere Americana, this book is a direct appeal for world governments to help the hardest-hit victims of natural disasters create new and better lives for themselves. Guthrie contrives to let his readers know in subtle ways that capitalism is the real villain in the Great Depression. It's reasonable to say that Guthrie's novel could just as easily have been set in a Haitian shanty-town or a Sudanese refugee camp as in Texas.

2

It was desperation that first brought Guthrie to forlorn Pampa. He had been born on July 14, 1912, in Okemah, Oklahoma, but in 1927, after Woody's mother was sent to Central State Hospital for the Insane in Norman (for what today would be diagnosed as Huntington's disease), his father moved to the Texas Panhandle. Not only were the crops withered in the Oklahoma fields during the 1920s, but the oil fields were also drying up. Tragedy seemed to follow young Woody around like a thundercloud: his older sister, Clara, died in a fire in 1919; then a decade later the Great Depression hit the Great Plains hard, bringing widespread poverty and further dislocation. After spending much of his teens scraping out an existence in Oklahoma, Woody decided in 1929 to join his father in Pampa, a far-flung community in the Texas Panhandle populated largely by cowboys, merchants, itinerant day laborers, and farmers. The mostly self-educated Woody, who had taken to playing the guitar and harmonica for a living, married a Pampa girl, Mary Jennings, who was the younger sister of a friend, the musician Matt Jennings. They would have three children. An oil discovery in the mid-1920s unexpectedly turned Pampa into a boomtown. The Guthries ran a boardinghouse, hoping to capitalize on the prosperity.

Temperamentally unsuited to a sunup-to-sundown job, Guthrie—a slight man weighing only 125 pounds—played a handsome mandolin for tips or sandwiches in every dark juke joint, dance hall, cantina, gin mill, and *tequilería* from Amarillo to Tucumcari. Leftist and progressive-minded, Guthrie was determined not to let poverty beat him down. He considered himself a straight-talking advocate for truth and love like Will Rogers. With head cocked and chin up, he embodied the authentic West Texas drifter complaining about how rotten life was for the poor. He became a singing spokesman for the impoverished, the debt-ridden, and the socially ostracized. Comic absurdity, however, infused everything Guthrie did. "We played for rodeos, centennials, carnivals, parades, fairs, just bustdown parties," Guthrie recalled, "and played several nights and days a week just to hear our own boards rattle and our strings roar around in the wind."

Determined to be a good father to his first daughter, Gwendolyn, Guthrie tried to earn an honest living in Pampa. But he was restless and broke. For extra money, he painted signs for the local C and C Market. When not making music or drawing, he holed up in the Pampa Public Library; the librarian there said he had a voracious appetite for books. Longing to grapple with life's biggest questions, he joined the Baptist church, studied faith healing and fortune-telling, read Rosicrucian tracts, and dabbled in Eastern philosophy.

He opened for business as a psychic in hopes of helping locals with their personal problems. He wanted to be a fulfiller of dreams. His music, grounded in his dedication to improving the lives of the downtrodden, was sometimes broadcast on weekends from a shoe box–size radio station in Pampa. Depending on his mood at any moment, he could be a cornpone comedian or a profound country philosopher of the airwaves. But he was always pure Woody.

His tramps around Texas took him south to the Permian basin, east to the Houston-Galveston area, then up through the Brazos valley into the North Central Plains, and back to the oil fields around Pampa. Always pulling for the underdog, the footloose Guthrie lived in hobo camps, using his meager earnings to buy meals or to shower. He was proud to be part of the downtrodden of the southern zone. His heart swelled with his new social consciousness:

> *If I was President Roosevelt*
> *I'd make groceries free—*
> *I'd give away new Stetson hats,*
> *And let the whiskey be.*
> *I'd pass out suits of clothing*
> *At least three times a week—*
> *And shoot the first big oil man*
> *That killed the fishing creek.*

It was while busking around New Mexico that Guthrie's gospel of adobe took root. In December 1936, nineteen

months after the Black Sunday when the dust storm ter-
rorized the Texas Panhandle, Guthrie had an epiphany.
In Santa Fe he visited a Nambé pueblo on the outskirts
of town. The mud-daubed adobe walls fascinated him (as
they had D. H. Lawrence and Georgia O'Keeffe). The
adobe haciendas had hardy wooden rainspouts and bricks
of soil and straw that were simple yet perfectly weatherproof, unlike most of the homes of his Texas friends,
which were poorly constructed with scrap lumber and
cheap nails. These New Mexico adobe homes, with their
mud bricks (ten inches wide, fourteen inches long, and
four inches high) baked in the sun, Guthrie understood,
were built to last the ages.

Adobe was one of the first building materials ever used
by man. Guthrie believed that Jesus Christ—his savior—
was born in an adobe manger. Such structures seemed to
signify Mother Earth herself. If the people in towns like
Pampa were going to survive dust storms and snow blizzards, Guthrie decided, they would have to build Nambé-
style homes that would stand stoutly until the Second
Coming of Christ. In New Mexico, with almost religious
zeal, he started painting adobes of "open air, clay, and sky."
In front of the Santa Fe Art Museum one afternoon, an old
woman told Guthrie, "The world is made of adobe." He was
transfixed by her comment but managed to nod his head in
agreement and reply, "So is man."

Out of these epiphanies in New Mexico was born the
central premise of *House of Earth*. To Guthrie, New Mexico,

the Land of Enchantment, was a crossroads of Hispanic, Native American, African American, Asian, and European cultures. He thought of the state as a mosaic of enduring peoples and cultures. Taos Pueblo—some of its structures as much as five stories high—had been occupied by Native Americans without interruption for a millennium. Santa Fe, founded in 1610, was the first and longest-lasting European capital on US soil. As Guthrie wrote in his song "Bling Blang"—which he recorded for his 1956 album *Songs to Grow On for Mother and Child*—his day of reckoning, with regard to New Mexico–style adobe, was fast approaching.

> *I'll grab some mud and you grab some clay*
> *So when it rains it won't wash away.*
> *We'll build a house that'll be so strong,*
> *The winds will sing my baby a song.*

From his inquiries in New Mexico, Guthrie learned that you didn't have to be a trained mason to build an adobe home. His dream was to live and wander in the Texas Panhandle, and to build a lasting adobe sanctuary on the ranch land he could return to at any time—one that wasn't a wooden coffin or owned by a bank or vulnerable to the dreaded dust and snow. With the well-reasoned conviction, Guthrie, voice of the rain-starved Dust Bowl, started preaching back in Texas about the utilitarian value of adobe. For five cents, he purchased from the USDA its Bulletin No. 1720, *The Use of Adobe or Sun-Dried Brick for Farm Building*.

Written by T. A. H. Miller, this how-to manual taught poor rural folks (among others) how to build an adobe from the cellar up. In the Panhandle, there was no cheap lumber or stone available, so adobe was the best bet for architecturally sound homes in the Southwest. All an amateur needed was a homemade mixture of clay loam and straw, which helped the brick to dry and shrink as a unit. Constructing a leak-proof roof was really the only difficult part. (Emulsified asphalt was eventually used to seal the roofs of adobes.) The rest was as easy as playing tic-tac-toe.

The model US city in the pamphlet was Las Cruces, New Mexico, where 80 percent of all structures were made of adobe. Guthrie promoted this USDA guide for decades. Realizing that dugouts in the Panhandle had endured the Dust Bowl better than wooden aboveground structures, which were vulnerable to wind and termites, Guthrie considered it a public service to promote the notion of adobe dwellings in drought areas. If sharecroppers and tenant farmers in places like Pampa could only own a piece of land—even unculti-vable land among arroyos or red rocks—they could build a dream "house of earth" that was fireproof, sweatproof, windproof, snowproof, Dust Bowl–proof, thiefproof, and bugproof.

It was early in January 1937 that Guthrie's vision of adobe inspired *House of Earth*. A vicious blizzard, in which dust mixed with snow to turn the white flakes brown, hit the Panhandle, and Guthrie's miserable twenty-five-dollar-a-month shack rattled in what the *Pampa Daily News* deemed the most "freakish" storm ever. Never before had residents experienced a summer storm, complete with thunder and lightning, in subzero temperatures. Sitting by the fireplace— the thermostat having frozen—Guthrie dreamed of warm adobes and started plotting *House of Earth*. In Los Angeles the previous year, Guthrie had befriended the actor and social activist Eddie Albert (who would make his feature film debut in Hollywood's 1938 version of *Brother Rat* with Ronald Reagan and would star in the CBS television sitcom *Green Acres* from 1965 to 1971). Guthrie had been so taken with the charismatic Albert, a proponent of organic farming, that he had given Albert his guitar as a going-away gift. "Well howdy," Guthrie now wrote to Albert from frigid Pampa. "We didn't have no trouble finding the dustbowl, and are about as covered up as one family can get. Only trouble is the dust is so froze up it cain't blow, so it just scrapes around. Had seven or eight fair sized blizzards down here. But was 3 or 4 days a having them. It run us out of our front room the last freeze. We had the cook stove and the heater a going full blast in the house and it was so windy inside it nearly blowed the fires out. We dig in at night and out about sunup. This one has really been a freezeout. Snowed and thawed out 3 times while we was hanging out the clothes. They froze on the line. We took em down just like boards."

The mercury dropped to six degrees below zero in Pampa, and gas lines froze, leaving homes without heat. While Guthrie was glad to be back home in Pampa—even in wintertime—he was a worried man. What the *New York*

Times called a "blizzard of frozen mud" the color of "cocoa" was pummeling the Great Plains. In Pampa, visibility was often less than two hundred feet. Stuck in his shack, bitterly cold and trying to keep his baby girl from catching a fever, Guthrie fantasized about handcrafting adobe bricks come the spring thaw. Such a bold venture would cost him $300 for supplies for a six-room residence. "You dig you a cellar and mix the mud and straw right in there, sorta with your feet, you know, and you get the mud just the right thickness and you put it in a mould, and you mould out around 20 bricks a day, and in a reasonable length of time you have got enough to build your house," he wrote to Albert. "You kinda let the weather cure em for around 2 or 3 weeks and the sun bakes em, then you raise up your wall."

Guthrie's letter to Eddie Albert—previously unpublished, like *House of Earth* itself—is a recent discovery. It illuminates how mesmerized Guthrie was by the vision of his own adobe home while trying to survive the brutal winter of 1937.

We sent off to Washington DC and get us back a book about sun dried brick.

Them guys up there around that Dept of Agriculture knows a right smart. They can write about work and make you think you got a job.

They wrote that Adobe Brick book so dadgum interesting that you got to slack up every couple of pages to pull the mud and hay out from between your toes.

INTRODUCTION

People around here for some reason aint got much faith in a adobe mud house. Old Timers dont seem to think it would stand up. But this here Dept of Agr. Book has got a map there in it which shows what parts of the country the dirt will work and tells in no hidden words that sun dried brick is the answer to many a dustblown familys prayer.

Since by a lot of hard work, which us dustbowlers are long on, and a very small cash cost, any family can raise a dern good house which is bug proof, fireproof, and cool in summer, and not windy inside in the winter.

I have been sort of experimenting out here in the yard with mud bricks, and after you make a bunch of em, you'd say yourself if a fellow caint raise up a house out of dust and water, by George, he caint raise it up out of nothing.

Right on hand I got a good cement man when he can get work and also a uncle of mine thats lived up here on the plains for 45 years, and he knows all of these hills and hollers and breaks in the land and canyons, and river bottoms where we can get stuff to built with, like timber and rock and sand, and he's too old to get a job but just the right age to build.

This cement workers is just right freshly married. But could work some.

Now since this climate is fairly dry and mighty dusty, and in view of the wind that blows, and the wheat that somehow grows, why hadn't these good cheap houses be introduced around here, which by the bricks in my back yard, I think is a big success.

If folks caint find no work at nothing else they can build em a house. There is plenty of exercise to it.

We've owned this little wood house for six years and it has been a blessing over and over, and the same amount of work and money spent on this house will raise one just exactly twice this good from the very well advertised dust of the earth.

It would be nearly dustproof, and a whole lot warmer, and last longer to boot. But folks around here just havent studied it out, or got no information from the government, or somehow are walking around over and overlooking their own salvation.

Local lumber yards dont advertize mud and straw because you cant find a spot on earth without it, but you see old adobe brick houses almost everywhere that are as old as Hitlers tricks, and still standing, like the Jews.

If I was aiming to preach you a sermon on the subject I would get a good lungful of air and say that man is himself a adobe house, some sort of a streamlined old temple.

But what I want to come around to before the paper runs out is this: We're scratching our heads about where to raise this $300 and we would furnish the labor and work, and we would write up a note of some kind a telling that this house belonged to somebody else till we could pay it out. . . .

*Course the payments would have to run pretty low till
we could get strung out and the weather thaw out and the
sun take a notion to come out, but it would be a loan and
as welcome as a gift.*

*In this case, a few retakes on the lenders part could
shore change a mighty bleak picture into a good one, and
maybe an endless One.*

Starting in the late 1930s, Guthrie toyed with the idea
of writing a panegyric to survivors of the Dust Bowl with
adobe as the leitmotif. Because John Steinbeck had sto-
len his thunder by writing *The Grapes of Wrath*, about the
Okie migration westward from Oklahoma and Texas to
California, Guthrie decided to focus instead on his own
authentic experience as a survivor of Black Sunday and the
great mud blizzard. Also, to his ears, the dialect of Steinbeck's uprooted Joads fell short of realism. To Guthrie,
true-to-life bad grammar was the essential way to capture
the spirit of how people *really* talked on the frontier. Like
Joel Chandler Harris, the author of the Uncle Remus tales,
he was an excellent listener. So *House of Earth*, in Guthrie's
mind, would be less an adulterated documentation of the
meteorological calamities than a pioneering work in capturing Texas-Okie dialects. Steinbeck, like all reporters,
focused on the dust cyclones, but Guthrie knew that the
frigid winter storms in West Texas during the Dust Bowl
era also crippled his fellow plainsmen. Guthrie granted
Steinbeck the diploma for documenting the diaspora to

California. Nevertheless, he himself claimed for literature those brave and stubborn souls who decided to stay put in the Texas Panhandle. It was one thing for Steinbeck, in *The Grapes of Wrath*, to feature families who were searching for a land of milk and honey, but Guthrie's own heart was with those stubborn dirt farmers who remained behind in the Great Plains to stand up to the bankers, lumber barons, and agribusinesses that had desecrated beautiful wild Texas with overgrazing, clear-cutting, strip-mining, and reckless farming practices. The gouged land and the working folks got diddly-squat . . . nothing . . . zero . . . nada . . . zilch. (For a while Guthrie used the nom de plume Alonzo Zilch.)

While Guthrie's twenty-five-year-old heart stayed in Texas, his legs would soon be bound for California. Much like Tike Hamlin, the main character in *House of Earth*, Guthrie paced the floorboards of his hovel at 408 South Russell Street in Pampa during the great mud blizzard of 1937, wondering how to find meaning in the drought-stricken misery of the Depression. His salvation required a choice: to go to California or to build an adobe homestead in Texas. When the character Ella May Hamlin screams, "Why has there got to be always something to knock you down? Why is this country full of things you can't see, things that beat you down, kick you down, throw you around, and kill out your hope?" the reader feels that Guthrie is expressing his own deep-seated frustration. He decided he would have to try his luck in California if he wanted a steady income. Having learned the Carter Family's old-style country tunes, and with original songs like "Ramblin' Round" and "Blowing Down This Old Dusty Road" in his repertoire, he was determined to become a folksinger who mattered. In early 1937—the exact week is unknown, but it was after the snow had thawed—Guthrie packed up his painting supplies, put new strings on his guitar, and bummed a ride in a beer delivery truck to Groom, Texas. Hopping out of the cab and waving good-bye, he started hitching down Highway 66 (what Steinbeck called the "road of flight"), where migrants were begging for food in every flyspeck town, to Los Angeles.

There is an almost biblical sense of trials and tribulations in the obstacles Guthrie would confront in California. Like all the other migrants on Highway 66, he always felt starvation banging on his rib cage. From time to time, he pawned his guitar to buy food. Like the photographer Dorothea Lange, he visited farm camps in California's San Joaquin Valley, stunned to see so many children suffering from malnutrition. But then Guthrie's big break came when he landed a job as an entertainer on KFVD radio in Los Angeles, singing "old-time" traditional songs with his partner Maxine Crissman ("Lefty Lou from Mizzou"). His hillbilly demeanor was affecting, and the local airwaves allowed Guthrie to reach fellow workers in migrant camps with his nostalgic songs about life in Oklahoma and Texas. For a while, he broadcast out of the XELO studio from Villa Acuña in the Mexican state of Coahuila; the station's powerful signal went all over the American Midwest and Canada, unimpeded by topography and unfettered by FCC regulations.

Many radio station owners wanted Guthrie to be a smooth cowboy swing crooner like Bob Wills ("My Adobe Hacienda") and Gene Autry ("Back in the Saddle Again"). Guthrie, however, had developed a different strategy for folksinging that he clung to uncompromisingly. "I hate a song that makes you think you're not any good," he explained. "I hate a song that makes you think that you are just born to lose. Bound to lose. No good to nobody. No good for nothing. Because you are either too old or too young or too fat or too slim or too ugly or too this or too that . . . songs that run you down or songs that poke fun of you on account of your bad luck or your hard traveling. I am out to fight those kinds of songs to my very last breath of air and my last drop of blood."

When Guthrie became a "hobo reporter" for *The Light* in 1938, he traveled extensively, reporting on the 1.25 million displaced Americans of the late 1930s. The squalor of the migrant camps angered him. He kept wishing the poor could live in adobe homes. "People living hungrier than rats and dirtier than dogs," Guthrie wrote, "in the land of sun and a valley of night." Guthrie came to understand that, contrary to myth, these so-called Dust Bowl refugees hadn't been chased out of Texas by dusters; nor had they been made obsolete by large farm tractors. They were victims of banks and landlords who had evicted them simply for reasons of greed. These money-grubbers wanted to evict tenant farmers in order to turn a patchwork quilt of little farms into huge cattle conglomerates, and they thereby forced rural folks into poverty. During his travels around California, Guthrie saw migrants living in cardboard boxes, mildewed tents, filthy huts, and orange-crate shanties. Every flimsy structure known to mankind had been built, but adobe homes were nowhere to be found. This rankled Guthrie boundlessly. What would Jesus Christ think of these predatory money changers destroying the family farms of America and forcing good folks to live in wretched lean-tos? "For every farmer who was dusted out or tractored out," Guthrie said, "another ten were chased out by bankers."

The Franklin Roosevelt administration tried to help poor farmers through the federal Resettlement Administration (the successor to the Farm Security Administration, famous for collaborating with such artists as Dorothea Lange, Walker Evans, and Pare Lorentz) by issuing grants of ten to forty-five dollars a month to the down-and-out; farmers would line up at the Resettlement Administration offices for these grants. President Roosevelt also aimed to help farmers like the Hamlins by ordering the US Forest Service to plant millions of acres of trees and shrubs on farms to serve as shelterbelts (and reduce wind erosion) and by having the Department of Agriculture start digging lakes in Oklahoma and Texas to provide irrigation for the dry iron grass. These noble New Deal efforts helped but didn't completely solve the crisis.

3

The legend of Guthrie as a folksinger is etched in the collective consciousness of America. Compositions like "Deportee," "Pastures of Plenty," and "Pretty Boy Floyd" became national treasures, like Benjamin Franklin's *Poor Richard's Almanack* and Mark Twain's *Adventures of Huckleberry Finn*. With the slogan "This Machine Kills Fascists" emblazoned on his guitar, Guthrie tramped around the country, a self-styled cowboy-hobo and jack-of-all-trades championing the underdog in his proletarian lyrics. When Guthrie heard Irving Berlin's "God Bless America" sung by Kate Smith ad nauseam in 1939, on radio stations from coast to coast, he decided to strike out against the lyrical rot and false comfort of the patriotic song. Holed up in Hanover House—a low-rent hotel on the corner of Forty-Third Street and Sixth Avenue—Guthrie wrote a rebuttal to "God Bless America" on February 23, 1940. He originally titled the song "God Blessed America" but eventually settled on "This Land Is Your Land." Because Guthrie saved thousands of his song lyrics in first and final drafts, we're lucky to still have the fourth and sixth verses of the ballad, pertaining to class inequality:

As I went walking, I saw a sign there,
*And on the sign there, it said "no trespassing."**
But on the other side, it didn't say nothing,
That side was made for you and me.

In the squares of the city, in the shadow of a steeple;
By the relief office, I'd seen my people.
As they stood there hungry, I stood there asking,
Is this land made for you and me?

Guthrie signed the lyric sheet, "All you can write is what you see, Woody G., N.Y., N.Y., N.Y." (During that week in Hanover House, the hyperproductive Guthrie also wrote "The Government Road," "Dirty Overhalls," "Will Rogers Highway," and "Hangknot Slipknot.")

Over the decades, "This Land Is Your Land" has become more a populist manifesto than a popular song. It's Guthrie's "The Times They Are a-Changin'," a call to arms. There is a hymnlike simplicity to Woody's signature tune. The lyric is clear and focused. Woody's art always reflected his political leanings, but that was all part of his *esprit*. He wasn't, in the end, a persona. What you heard was real as rain. There was no separation between song and singer.

Everything about a Guthrie song accentuated the positive in people struggling against all odds. He would trumpet hope at every turn. He even once referred to himself as a

---

* In one recorded version of the song he replaced "no trespassing" with the more anticapitalist "private property."

"hoping machine," in a letter when he was courting a future wife. Guthrie sought to empower those who had nothing, to uplift those who had lost everything in the Great Depression, and to comfort those who found themselves repeatedly at the mercy of Mother Nature. He could not help raging at the swinish injustice of it all, in the two fierce verses in "This Land Is Your Land" that slammed private property and food shortages—verses that were lost during the period of McCarthy's "red scare." A relatively unknown, but very important, verse—"Nobody living can ever stop me . . . Nobody living can ever make me turn back"—challenges the agents of the authoritarian state who prevent free access to the land that was "made for you and me." Reading all the verses now, one is impressed by Guthrie's ability to elucidate such simple, brutal truths in such resolute words.

In many ways, *House of Earth*—originally handwritten in a steno notebook and then typed by Guthrie himself—is a companion piece to "This Land Is Your Land." It's another not-so-subtle paean to the plight of Everyman. After all, in a socialist utopia, once a Great Plains family acquired land, it would need to build a sturdy domicile on the property. The novel is therefore pitched somewhere between rural realism and proletarian protest, with a static narrative but a lovely portrait of the Panhandle and the marginalized people who made a life there in the 1930s. It's Guthrie addressing the elemental question of how a sharecropper couple, field hands, could best live in a Dust Bowl–prone West Texas. Trapped in adverse economic conditions, unable to pay their bills or earn anything more than a subsistence wage, Guthrie's main characters dream of a better way. Tike Hamlin—like Guthrie himself—wants to build an adobe home for his family. Wherever Guthrie went, no matter the day or time, he talked about someday having his own adobe home. "I am stubborn as the devil, want to built it my own self," Guthrie wrote to a friend in 1947, "with my own hands and my own labors out of pisse de terra sod, soil, and rock and clay."

Before writing *House of Earth*, he had composed his autobiography, *Bound for Glory*, in the early 1940s. In that work, Guthrie proved to be a genius at capturing the rural Texas-Oklahoma dialect in realistic prose. Somehow he managed to straddle the line between "outsider" folk art and "insider" high art. *Bound for Glory*—which was made into a motion picture in 1976—is an impressive first try from an amateur inspired by native radicalism. Guthrie's great accomplishment was that his sui generis singing voice, his trademark, prospered in his prose.

Another book of Guthrie's, *Seeds of Man*—about a silver mine around Big Bend National Park in Texas—was largely a memoir, though fictionalized in parts. There is an authenticity about this book that was—and still is—ennobling. He saw his next prose project—*House of Earth*—as a heartfelt paean to rural poverty. (Just a month after Guthrie had written "This Land Is Your Land," he played the guitar and regaled his audience with stories about hard times in the Dust Bowl at a now legendary benefit for migrant workers hosted by the John Steinbeck Committee to Aid Agricultural Organization.)

What Guthrie wanted to explore in *House of Earth* was how places like Pampa could be something more than tumbleweed ghost towns, how sharecropping families could put down permanent roots in West Texas. He wanted to tackle such topics as overgrazing and the ecological threats inherent in fragmenting native habitats. He elucidated the need for class warfare in rural Texas, for a pitchfork rebellion of the 99 percent working folks against the 1 percent financiers. His outlook was socialistic. (Bricks to all landlords! Bankruptcy to all timber dealers! Curses on real estate maggots glutting themselves on the poor!) And he unapologetically announces that being a farmer is God's highest calling.

One of the main attractions of Guthrie's writing—and of *House of Earth* in particular—is our awareness that the author has personally experienced the privations he describes. Yet this is different from pure autobiography. Guthrie gets to the essence of poor folks without looking down on them from a higher perch like James Agee or Jacob Riis. His gritty realism is communal, expressing oneness with the subjects. The Hamlins, it seems, have more in common with the pioneers of the Oregon Trail than with a modern-day couple sleeping on rollout beds in Amarillo during the Internet age. Objects such as cowbells, oil stoves, flickering lamps, and orange-crate shelves speak of a bygone era when electricity hadn't yet made it to rural America. But while the atmosphere of *House of Earth* places the novel firmly in the Great Depression, the themes that Guthrie ponders—misery, worry, tears, fun, and lonesomeness—are as old as human history. Guthrie's aim is to remind readers that they are merely specks of dust in the long march forward from the days of the cavemen.

The Hamlins have a hard life in a flimsy wooden shack, yet exist with extreme (and emotionally fraught) vitality. The reader learns at the outset that their home is not up to the function of keeping out the elements. So Tike starts exasperatedly espousing the idealistic gospel of adobe. On the farm, life persists, and the reader is treated to an extended, earthy lovemaking scene. This intimate description serves a purpose: Guthrie elevates the biological act to a representation of Tike and Ella May's oneness with the land, the farm, and each other. And yet, the land is not the Hamlins' to do with as they please—and so the building of their adobe house remains painfully out of reach. The narrative then concerns itself with domestic interactions between Tike and Ella May. Despite their great energy and playfulness, dissatisfaction wells up in them. In the closing scenes, in which Ella May gives birth, we learn more about their financial woes and how tenant farmers lived on tenterhooks during the Great Depression when they had no property rights.

4

When the folklorist Alan Lomax read the first chapter of *House of Earth* ("Dry Rosin"), he was bowled over, amazed at how Guthrie expressed the emotions of the downtrodden with such realism and dignity. For months Lomax encouraged Guthrie to finish the book, saying that he'd "considered dropping everything I was doing" just to sell the novel. "It was quite simply," Lomax wrote, "the best material I'd ever seen written about that section of the country." *House of Earth* demonstrates that Guthrie's social conscience is comparable to Steinbeck's and that Guthrie, like D. H. Lawrence in *Lady Chatterley's Lover*, was willing to explore raw sexuality.

Guthrie apparently never showed Lomax the other three chapters of the novel: "Termites," "Auction Block," and "Hammer Ring." His hopes for *House of Earth* lay in Hollywood. He mailed the finished manuscript to the film-maker Irving Lerner, who had worked on such socially conscious documentaries as *One Third of a Nation* (1939), *Valley Town* (1940), and *The Land* (1941). Guthrie hoped that Lerner would make the novel into a low-budget feature film. This never came to pass. The book languished in obscurity. Only quite recently, when the University of Tulsa started assembling a Woody Guthrie collection, did *House of Earth* reemerge into the light. The Lerner estate had found the treasure when organizing its own archives in .

Los Angeles. The manuscript and a cache of letters written by Guthrie and Lerner to each other were promptly shipped to Tulsa's McFarlin Library for permanent housing. Coincidentally, while hunting down information about Bob Dylan for a *Rolling Stone* project, we stumbled on the novel. Like Lomax, we grew determined to have *House of Earth* published properly by a New York house, as Guthrie surely would have wanted.

The question has been asked: Why wasn't *House of Earth* published in the late 1940s? Why would Guthrie work so furiously on a novel and then let it die on the vine? There are a few possible answers. Most probably, he was hoping a movie deal might emerge; that took patience. Perhaps Guthrie sensed that some of the content was passé (the fertility cycle trope, for example, was frowned on by critics) or that the sexually provocative language was ahead of its time (graphic sex of the "stiff penis" variety was not yet acceptable in literature during the 1940s). The lovemaking between Tike and Ella May is a brave bit of emotive writing and an able exploration of the psychological dynamics of intercourse. But it's a scene that, in the age when *Tropic of Cancer* was banned, would have been misconstrued as pornographic. Another impediment to publication may have been Guthrie's employment of hillbilly dialect. This perhaps made it difficult for New York literary circles to embrace *House of Earth* as high art in the 1940s, though the dialect comes across as noble in our own period of linguistic archaeology. Also, left-leaning originality was hard to mass-market in the Truman era, when Soviet communism was public enemy number one. And critics at the time were bound to dismiss the novel's enthusiasm for southwestern adobe as fetishistic.

Toward the end of *House of Earth*, Tike rails against the sheeplike mentality of honest folks in Texas and Oklahoma who let low-down capitalist vultures steal from them. Long before Willie Nelson and Neil Young championed "Farm Aid," a movement of the 1980s to stop industrial agriculture from running amok on rural families, Guthrie worried about middle-class folks who were being robbed by greedy banks. As Tike prepares to make love to Ella May in the barn scene in *House of Earth*, his head swirls with thoughts of how everything around him—"house, barn, the iron water tank, the windmill, little henhouse, the old Ryckzyck shack, the whole farm, the whole ranch"—was "a part of him, the same as an egg from the farm went into his mouth and down his throat and was a part of him." Tike is biologically one with even the hay on his leased property.

In 1947, after years of gestation, *House of Earth* was finished. Shortly thereafter Guthrie's health started to deteriorate from complications of Huntington's disease. While disciples like Ramblin' Jack Elliott and Pete Seeger popularized his folk repertoire, *House of Earth* remained among Lerner's papers. Like a mural by Thomas Hart Benton or a novel by Erskine Caldwell, it was an artifact from a different era: it didn't fit into any of the standard categories of popular fiction during the Cold War. But, as Guthrie might say, "All good things in due time." The unerring rightness of southwestern adobe living is now more apparent than ever. Oscar Wilde was right: "Literature always anticipates life." It's almost as if Guthrie had written *House of Earth* prophetically, with global warming in mind.

To read the voice of Guthrie is to hear the many voices of the people, his people, those hardworking Great Plains folks who didn't have a platform from which their sharp anguish could be heard. His voice was the pure expression of the lost, of the downtrodden, of the forgotten American who scratched out a living from the heartland.

While Guthrie was himself a common man, he was uncommon in his efforts to celebrate the proletariat in his art. He hoped someday Americans could learn how to abolish the laws of debt and repayment. Guthrie wanted to be heard, to count for something. He demanded that his political beliefs be acknowledged, respected, and treated with dignity. As his graphic love scenes demonstrate, he wasn't scared of anyone. He had no fear. He lived his art. In short, Guthrie inspired not only people of his time, but people of later times enraged by injustice, yearning for truth, searching for that elusive resolution of class inequality.

We consider the publication of *House of Earth* an integral part of the celebration of the centennial of Woody Guthrie's birth, a significant cultural event, and a major installment in the corpus of his published work. He wrote the novel as a side project; it was never the focus of his intrepid life of performing his songs from coast to coast. Yet the novel's intensity guarantees it a place in the ever-growing field of Guthrieana. When we shared Guthrie's *House of Earth* with Bob Dylan, he said he was "surprised by the genius" of the engaging prose, a realistic meditation about how poor people search for love and meaning in a corrupt world where the rich have lost their moral compass.

The discovery of *House of Earth* reinforces Guthrie's place among the immortal figures of American letters. Guthrie endures as the soul of rural American folk culture in the twentieth century. His music is the soil. His words—lyrics, memoirs, essays, and now fiction—are the adobe bricks. He is of the people, by the people, for the people. Long may his truth be heard by all those who care to listen, all those with hope in their heart and strength in their stride. Guthrie's proletariat-troubadour legacy is profoundly human, and his work should be forever celebrated. As Steinbeck wrote in tribute, "Woody is just Woody. Thousands of people do not know he has any other name. He is just a voice and a guitar. He sings the songs of a people and I suspect that he is, in a way, that people. Harsh voiced and nasal, his guitar hanging like a tire iron on a rusty rim, there is nothing sweet about Woody, and there is nothing sweet about the songs he sings. But there is something more important for those who still listen. There is the will of a people to endure and fight against oppression. I think we call this the American spirit."

Douglas Brinkley and Johnny Depp
Albuquerque, New Mexico

HOUSE OF EARTH

DRY ROSIN

The wind of the upper flat plains sung a high lonesome song down across the blades of the dry iron grass. Loose things moved in the wind but the dust lay close to the ground.

It was a clear day. A blue sky. A few puffy, white-looking thunderclouds dragged their shadows like dark sheets across the flat Cap Rock country. The Cap Rock is that big high, crooked cliff of limestone, sandrock, marble, and flint that divides the lower west Texas plains from the upper north panhandle plains. The canyons, dry wash rivers, sandy creek beds, ditches, and gullies that joined up with the Cap Rock cliff form the graveyard of past Indian civilizations, flying and testing grounds of herds of leather-winged bats, drying grounds of monster-size bones and teeth, roosting, nesting, and the breeding place of the bald-headed big brown eagle. Dens of rattlesnakes, lizards, scorpions, spiders, jackrabbit, cottontail, ants, horny butterfly, horned toad, and stinging winds and seasons. These things all were born of the Cap Rock cliff and it was alive and moving with all these and with the mummy skeletons of early settlers of all colors. A world close to the sun, closer to the wind, the cloudbursts, floods, gumbo muds, the dry and dusty things that lose their footing in this world, and blow, and roll, jump wire fences, like the tumbleweed, and take their last earthly leap in the north wind out and down, off the upper north plains, and down onto the sandier cotton plains that commence to take shape west of Clarendon.

A world of big stone twelve-room houses, ten-room wood houses, and a world of shack houses. There are more of the saggy, rotting shack houses than of the nicer wood houses, and the shack houses all look to the larger houses and curse out at them, howl, cry, and ask questions about the rot, the filth, the hurt, the misery, the decay of land and of families. All kinds of fights break out between the smaller houses, the shacks, and the larger houses. And this goes for the town where the houses lean around on one another, and for the farms and ranch lands where the wind sports high, wide, and handsome, and the houses lay far apart. All down across this the wind blows. And the people work hard when the wind blows, and they fight even harder when the wind blows, and this is the canyon womb, the stickery bed, the flat pallet on the floor of the earth where the wind its own self was born.

The rocky lands around the Cap Rock cliff are mostly worn slick from suicide things blowing over it. The cliff itself, canyons that run into it, are banks of clay and layers of sand, deposits of gravel and flint rocks, sandstone, volcanic mixtures of dried-out lavas, and in some places the cliff wears a wig of nice iron grass that lures some buffalo, antelope, or beef steer out for a little bit, then slips out from underfoot, and sends more flesh and blood to the flies and the buzzards, more hot meals down the cliff to the white fangs of the coyote, the lobo, the opossum, coon, and skunk.

Old Grandpa Hamlin dug a cellar for his woman to keep her from the weather and the men. He dug it one half of one mile from the rim of Cap Rock cliff. He loved Della as much as he loved his land. He raised five of his boys and girls in the dugout. They built a yellow six-room house a few yards from the cellar. Four more children came in this yellow six-room house, and he took all of his children several trips down along the cliff rim, and pointed to the sky and said to them, "Them same two old eagles flyin' an' circlin' yonder, they was circlin' there on th' mornin' that I commenced to dig my dugout, an' no matter what hits you, kids, or no matter what happens to you, don't git hurried, don't git worried, 'cause the same two eagles will see us all come an' see us all go."

And Grandma Della Hamlin told them, "Get a hold of a piece of earth for yerself. Get a hold of it like this. And then fight. Fight to hold on to it like this. Wood rots. Wood decays. This ain't th' country to get a hold of nothin' made out of wood in. This ain't th' country of trees. This ain't even a country fer brush, ner even fer bushes. In this streak of th' land here you can't fight much to hold on to what's wood, 'cause th' wind an' th' sun, an' th' weather here's just too awful hard on wood. You can't fight your best unless you got your two feet on th' earth, an' fightin' fer what's made out of th' earth." And walking along the road that ran from the Cap Rock back to the home place, she would tell them, "My worst pain's always been we didn't raise up a house of earth 'stead of a house of wood. Our old dugout it was earth and it's outlived a hundred wood houses."

Still, the children one by one got married and moved apart. Grandma and Grandpa Hamlin could stand on the front porch of their old home place and see seven houses of their sons and daughters. Two had left the plains. One son moved to California to grow walnuts. A daughter moved to Joplin to live with a lead and zinc miner. Rocking back and forth in her chair on the porch, Della would say, "Hurts me, soul an' body, to look out acrost here an' see of my kinds a-livin' in those old wood houses." And Pa would smoke his pipe and watch the sun go down and say, "Don't fret so much about 'em, Del, they just take th' easy way. Cain't see thirty years ahead of their noses."

Tike Hamlin's real name was Arthur Hamlin. Della and Pa had called him Little Tyke on the day that he was born, and he had been Tike Hamlin ever since. The brand of Arthur was frozen into a long icicle and melted into the sun, gone and forgotten, and not even his own papa and mama thought of Arthur except when some kind of legal papers had to be signed or something like that.

Tike was the only one of the whole Hamlin tribe that was not born up on top of the Cap Rock. There was a little oblong two-room shack down in a washout canyon where his mama had planted several sprigs of wild yellow plum bushes near the doorstep. She dug up the plum roots and chewed on them for snuff sticks, and she used the chewed sticks to brush her teeth. The shack fell down so bad that she got afraid of snakes, lizards, flies, bugs, gnats, and howling coyotes, and argued her husband into building a five-room house on six hundred and forty acres of new wheat land just one mile due north, on a straight line, from the old Pa Hamlin dugout.

Tike was a medium man, medium wise and medium ignorant, wise in the lessons taught by fighting the weather and working the land, wise in the tricks of the men, women, animals, and all of the other things of nature, wise to guess a blizzard, a rainstorm, dry spell, the quick change of the hard wind, wise as to how to make friends, and how to fight enemies. Ignorant as to the things of the schools. He was a wiry, hard-hitting, hardworking sort of a man. There was no extra fat around his belly because he burned it up faster than it could grow there. He was five feet and eight inches tall, square built, but slouchy in his actions, hard of muscle, solid of bone and lungs, but with a good wide streak of laziness somewhere in him. He was of the smiling, friendly, easygoing, good-humored brand, but used his same smile to fool if he hated you, and grinned his same little grin even when he got the best or the worst end of a fistfight. As a young boy, Tike had all kinds of fights over all matters and torn off all kinds of clothes and come home with all kinds of cuts and bruises. But now he was in this thirty-third year, and a married man; his wife, Ella May, had taught him not to fight and tear up five dollars' worth of clothes unless he had a ten-dollar reason.

His hard work came over him by spells and his lazy dreaming came over him to cure his tired muscles. He was a dreaming man with a dreaming land around him, and a man of ideas and of visions as big, as many, as wild, and as orderly as the stars of the big dark night around him. His hands were large, knotty, and big boned, skin like leather, and the signs of his thirty-three years of salty sweat were carved in his wrinkles and veins. His hands were scarred, covered with old gashes, the calluses, cuts, burns, blisters that come from winning and losing and carrying a heavy load.

Ella May was thirty-three years old, the same age as Tike. She was small, solid of wind and limb, solid on her two feet, and a fast worker. She was a woman to move and to move fast and to always be on the move. Her black hair dropped down below her shoulders and her skin was the color of windburn. She woke Tike up out of his dreams two or three times a day and scolded him to keep moving. She seemed to be made out of the same stuff that movement itself is made of. She was energy going somewhere to work. Power going through the world for her purpose. Her two hands hurt and ached and moved with a nervous pain when there was no work to be done.

Tike ran back from the mailbox waving a brown envelope in the wind. "'S come! Come! Looky! Hey! Elly Mayyy!" He skidded his shoe soles on the hard ground as he ran up into the yard. "Lady!"

The ground around the house was worn down smooth, packed hard from footprints, packed still harder from the rains, and packed still harder from the soapy wash water that had been thrown out from tubs and buckets. A soapy coat of whitish wax was on top of the dirt in the yard, and it had soaked down several inches into the earth at some spots. The strong smell of acids and lyes came up to meet Ella May's nose as she carried two heavy empty twenty-gallon cream cans across the yard.

"Peeewwweee." She frowned up toward the sun, then across the cream cans at Tike, then back at the house. "Stinking old hole."

"Look." Tike put the envelope into her hand. "Won't be stinky long."

"Why? What's going to change it so quick all at once? Hmmm?" She looked down at the letter. "Hmmmm. United States Department of Agriculture. Mmmmm. Come on. We've got four more cream cans to carry from the windmill. I've been washing them out."

"Look inside." He followed her to the mill and rested his chin on her shoulder. "Inside."

"Grab yourself two cream cans, big boy."

"Look at th' letter."

"I'm not going to stop my work to read no letter from

nobody, especially from no old Department of Agriculture. Besides, my hands are all wet. Get those two cans there and help me to put them over on that old bench close to the kitchen window."

"Kitchen window? We ain't even got no kitchen." Tike caught hold of the handles of two of the cans and carried them along at her side. "Kitchen. Bull shit."

"I make out like it's my kitchen." She bent down at the shoulders under the weight of the cans. "Close as we'll ever get to one, anyhow." A little sigh of tired sadness was in her voice. Her words died down and the only sound was that of their shoe soles against the hard earth, and over all a cry that is always in these winds. "Whewww."

"Heavy? Lady?" He smiled along at her side and kept his eye on the letter in her apron pocket.

The wind was stiff enough to lift her dress up above her knees.

"You quit that looking at me, Mister Man."

"Ha, ha."

"You can see that I've got my hands full of these old cream cans. I can't help it. I can't pull it down."

"Free show. Free show," Tike sang out to the whole world as the wind showed him the nakedness of her thighs.

"You mean old thing, you."

"Hey, cows. Horses. Pugs. Piggeeee. Free show. Hey."

"Mean. Ornery."

"Hyeeah, Shep. Hyeah, Ring. Chick, chick, chick, chick,

chickeeee. Kitty, kitty, kitty, meeeooowww. Meeeooowww. Blow, Mister Wind! I married me a wife, and she don't even want me to see her legs! Blow!" He dug his right elbow into her left breast.

"Tike."

"Blowww!"

"Tike! Stop. Silly. Nitwit."

"Blowwww!" He rattled his two cans as he lifted them up onto the bench. In order to be polite, he reached to take hers and to set them up for her, but she steered out of his reach.

"You're downright vulgar. You're filthy-minded. You're just about the meanest, orneriest, no-accountest one man that I ever could pick out to marry! Looking at me that a way. Teasing me. That's just what you are. An old mean teaser. Quit that! I'll set my own cans on the bench." She lifted her cans.

"Lady." The devil of hell was in his grin.

"Don't. Don't you try to lady me." Her face changed from a half smile into a deep and tender hurt, a hurt that was older, and a hurt that was bigger than her own self. "This whole house here is just like that old rotten fell-down bench there. That old screen it's going to just dry up and blow to smithereens one of these days."

"Let it blow." Tike held a dry face.

"The wood in this whole window here is so rotten that it won't hold a nail anymore." Tears swept somewhere into her eyes as she bit her upper lip and sobbed, "I tried to tack the screen on better to keep those old biting flies out, and they just kept coming on in, because the wood was so rotten that the tacks fell out in less than twenty minutes."

Tike's face was sad for a second, but before she turned her eyes toward him, he slapped himself in the face with the back of his hand, in a way that always made him smile, glad or sad. "Let it be rotten, Lady." He put his hands on his hips and took a step backward, and stood looking the whole house over. "Guess it's got a right to be rotten if it wants to be rotten, Lady. Goldern whizzers an' little jackrabbits! Look how many families of kids that little ole shack has suckled up from pups. I'd be all rickety an' bowlegged, an' bent over, an' sagged down, an' petered out, an' swayed in my middle, too, if I'd stood in one little spot like this little ole shack has, an' stood there for fifty-two years. Let it rot. Rot! Rot down! Fall down! Sway in! Keel over! You little ole rotten piss soaked bastard, you! Fall!" His voice changed from one of good fun into words of raging terror. "Die! Fall! Rot!"

"I just hate it." She stepped backward and stood close up against him. "I work my hands and fingers down to the bones, Tike, but I can't make it any cleaner. It gets dirtier every day."

Tike's hand felt the nipples of her breast as he kissed her on the neck from behind and chewed her gold earrings between his teeth. His fingers rubbed her breasts, then rubbed her stomach as he pulled the letter out of her apron pocket. "Read th' little letter?"

"Hmh? Just look at those poor old rotted-out boards. You can actually see them rot and fall day after day." She leaned back against his belt buckle.

He put his arms around her and squeezed her breasts soft and easy in his hands. He held his chin on her right shoulder and smelled the skin of her neck and her hair as they both stood there and looked.

"Department of Agriculture." She read on the outside.

"Uh-hmm."

"Why. A little book. Let's see. Farmer's Bulletin Number Seventeen Hundred. And Twenty. Mm-hmm."

"Yes, ma'am."

"The Use of Adobe or Sun Dried Brick for Farm Building." A smile shone through her tears.

"Yes, Lady." He felt her breasts warmer under his hands.

"A picture of a house built out of adobe. All covered over with nice colored stucco. Pretty. Well, here's all kinds of drawings, charts, diagrams, showing just about everything in the world about it."

"How to build it from th' cellar up. Free material. Just take a lot of labor an' backbendin'," he said. Then a smile was in his soul. "Cost me a whole big nickel, that book did."

"Adobe. Or Sun-Dried Brick. For Farm Building." She flipped into the pages and spoke a few slow words. "It is fireproof. It is sweatproof. It does not take skilled labor. It is windproof. It can't be eaten up by termites."

"Wahooo!"

"It is warm in cold weather. It is cool in hot weather. It is easy to keep fresh and clean. Several of the oldest houses in the country are built out of earth." She looked at the picture of the nice little house and flowers on the front of the book. "All very well. Very, very well. But."

"But?" he said in a tough way. "But?"

"But. Just one or two buts." She pooched her lips as her eyes dropped down along the ground. "You see that stuff there, that soil there under your feet?"

"Sure." Tike looked down. "I see it. 'Bout it?"

"That is the but."

"The but? Which but? Ain't no buts to what that book there says. That's a U.S. Gover'ment book, an' it's got th' seal right there, there in that lower left-hand corner! What's wrong with this soil here under my foot? It's as hard as 'dobey already!"

"But. But. But. It just don't happen to be your land." She tried hard and took a good bit of time to get her words out. Her voice sounded dry and raspy, nervous. "See, mister?"

Tike's hand rubbed his eye, then his forehead, then his hair, then the back of his neck, and his fingers pulled at the tip of his ear as he said, "'At's th' holdup."

"A house"—her voice rose—"of earth."

Tike only listened. His throat was so tight that no words could get out.

"A house of earth. And not an inch of earth to build it on." There was a quiver, a tremble, and a shake in her body as she scraped her shoe sole against the ground. "Oooo, yes," she said in a way that made fun of them both, of the whole farm, mocked the old cowshed, shamed the iron water tank, made fun of all the houses that lay within her sight. "Yesssss. We could build us up a mighty nice house of earth, if we could only get our hands on a piece of land. But. Well. That's where the mule throwed Tony."

"That's where th' mule"—he looked toward the sky, then down at the toe of his shoe—"throwed Tony."

She turned herself into a preacher, pacing up and down, back and forth, in front of Tike. She held her hands against her breasts, then waved them about, beat her fists in the wind, and spoke in a loud scream. "Why has there got to be always something to knock you down? Why is this country full of things that you can't see, things that beat you down, kick you down, throw you around, and kill out your hope? Why is it that just as fast as I hope for some little something or other, that some kind of crazy thievery always, always, always cuts me down? I'll not be treated any such way as this any longer, not one inch longer. Not one ounce longer, not one second longer. I never did in my whole life ask for one whit more than I needed. I never did ask to own, nor to rule, nor to control the lands nor the lives of other people. I never did crave anything except a decent chance to work, and a decent place to live, and a decent, honest life. Why can't we, Tike? Tell me. Why? Why can't we own enough land to keep us busy on? Why can't we own enough land to exist on, to work on, and to live on like human beings? Why can't we?"

Tike sat down in the sun and crossed his feet under him. He dug into the soapy dishwater dirt and said, "I don't know, Lady. People are just dog-eat-dog. They lie on one another, cheat one another, run and sneak and hide and count and cheat, and cheat, and then cheat some more. I always did wonder. I don't know. It's just dog-eat-dog. That's all I know."

She sat down in front of him and put her face down into his lap. And he felt the wet tears again on her cheeks. And she sniffed and asked him, "Why has it just got to be dog-eat-dog? Why can't we live so as to let other people live? Why can't we work so as to let other folks work? Dog-eat-dog! Dog-eat-dog! I'm sick and I'm tired, and I'm sick at my belly, and sick in my soul with this dog-eat-dog!"

"No sicker'n me, Lady. But don't jump on me. I didn't start it. I cain't put no stop to it. Not just me by myself." He held the back of her head in his hands.

"Oh. I know. I don't really mean that." She breathed her warm breath against his overalls as she sat facing him.

"Mean what?"

"Mean that you caused everybody to be so thieving and so low-down in their ways. I don't think that you caused it by yourself. I don't think that I caused it by myself, either. But I just think that both of us are really to blame for it."

"Us? Me? You?"

"Yes." She shook her head as he played with her hair. "I do. I really do."

"Hmmm."

"We're to blame because we let them steal," she told him.

"Let them? We caused 'em to steal?"

"Yes. We caused them to steal. Penny at a time. Nickel at a time. Dime. A quarter. A dollar. We were easygoing. We were good-natured. We didn't want money just for the sake of having money. We didn't want other folks' money if it meant that they had to do without. We smiled across their counters a penny at a time. We smiled in through their cages a nickel at a time. We handed a quarter out our front door. We handed them money along the street. We signed our names on their old papers. We didn't want money, so we didn't steal money, and we spoiled them, we petted them, and we humored them. We let them steal from us. We knew that they were hooking us. We knew it. We knew when they cheated us out of every single little red cent. We knew. We knew when they jacked up their prices. We knew when they cut down on the price of our work. We knew that. We knew they were stealing. We taught them to steal. We let them. We let them think that they could cheat us because we are just plain old common everyday people. They got the habit."

"They really got the habit," Tike said.

"Like dope. Like whiskey. Like tobacco. Like snuff. Like morphine or opium or old smoke of some kind. They got the regular habit of taking us for damned old silly fools," she said.

"You said a cuss word, Elly."

"I'll say worse than that before this thing is over with!"

"Naaa. Naaa. No more of that there cussin' outta you, now. I ain't goin' to set here an' listen to a woman of mine carry on in no such a way when she never did a cuss word in her whole life before."

"You'll hear plenty."

"I don't know why, Lady, never would know why, I don't s'pose. But them there cuss words just don't fit so good into your mouth. Me, it's all right for me to cuss. My old mouth has a little bit of ever'thing in it, anyhow. But no siree, not you. You're not goin' to lose your head an' start out to fightin' folks by cuss words. I'll not let you. I'll slap your jaws."

Ella May only shook her curls in his lap.

"You always could fight better by sayin' nice words, anyhow, Lady. I don't know how to tell you, but when I lose my nut an' go to cussin' out an' blowin' my top, seems like my words just get all out somewhere in th' wind, an' then they get lost, somehow. But you always did talk with more sense, somehow. Seems like that when you say somethin', somehow or another, it always makes sense, an' it always stays said. Cuts 'em deeper th'n my old loose flyin' cuss words."

"Cuts who?" She lifted her head and shook her hair back out of her face, and bit her lip as she tried to smile. "Who?"

"I don't know. All of them cheaters an' stealers you're talkin' about."

"I'm not talking about just any one certain man or

woman, Tike. I'm just talking about greed. Just plain old greed."

"Yeah. I know. Them greedy ones," he said.

And she said, "No. No. You know, Tike—ah, it may sound funny. But I think that the people that are greedy, well, they believe that it's right to be greedy. They've got a hope, a dream, a vision, inside of them just like I've, ah, we've got in us. And in a way it's pitiful, but it's not really their fault."

"Hmm?"

"No more than, say, a bad disease was to break out, like some kind of a fever, or some kind of a plague, and all of us would take it, all of us would get it. Some would have it very light, some would have it sort of, well, sort of medium. Others would have it harder and worse, and some would naturally have it bad. Some of us would lose our heads, and some would lose our hands, and some would lose our senses with the fever."

"Yeah. But who would be to blame for a plague? Cain't nobody start no fever nor a thing like a plague. Could they, Lady?"

"Filth causes diseases to eat people up."

"Yeah."

"And ignorance is the cause of people's filth."

"Yeah—but—"

"Don't *but* me. And ignorance is caused by your greed."

"My greed? You mean, ah, me? My greed? You mean that me, my greed caused this farm to be filthy? I didn't make it filthy. If it was mine, I'd clean th' damn thing up slicker'n a new hat."

She sat for a bit and looked out past his shoulder. "I feel the same way. I don't know. But you can't put your heart into anything if it's not your own."

"Shore cain't."

"I don't know. I never did know. But it looks like to me that we could get together and pass some laws that would give everybody, everybody enough of a piece of land to raise up a house on."

"Everybody would just go right straight and sell it to get some money to gamble with or to get drunk on, or to fuck with," he told her. "Gamble. Drink. Fuck."

"Should be fixed, though, to where if you went and sold your piece of land, then it went back into the hands of the Government, and not some old mean miserly money counter," she said.

"If th' Gover'ment was to pass out pieces of land right today, the banks would have it all back in two months." He laughed.

"And if that happened"—she tilted her head—"then the Government should take it away from the banks and pass it out all over again. What do we pay them for? Fishing."

"Fuckin'." Tike laughed again.

She half shut her eyes to get a good close look at his face and said, "Your mind is certainly on sex today."

"Ever'day."

"Every single sensible thing that I've said here about

your house of earth and your land to build it on, you've brought sex into it."

"What do you think I want a house an' a piece of land for, to concentrate in?"

"Don't your mind ever think about anything else except just getting a piece of lay?"

"Not that I recollect."

"How long has your mind been running thisaway?"

" 'Fore I learnt how to walk."

"Silly."

"Me silly? How come?"

"Oh." She looked at him. "I don't know. I guess you were just born sort of silly. How come you to be born so silly, anyhow? Tikey?"

"How come you to be born so perty? Lady?" Inside his overalls Tike felt the movement of his penis as it grew long and hard. In the way he was sitting there was not room enough for his penis to become stiff. His clothing caused it to bend in the middle in a way that dealt him a throbbing pain. He stood up on the ground and spread his legs apart. He reached inside his overalls with his fingers and put it in an upright position and sighed a breath of comfort. His blood ran warmer and the whole world seemed to be flying from under his feet. His old feeling was coming over him, and his eyes looked around the yard for something to say to Ella May.

She stood up and looked down at the ground where she had been sitting. She picked up the Department of Agricul-

ture book. Her eyes watched Tike as he held his hand inside his overalls. She saw his lips tremble and heard him inhale a deep lungful of air. "What have you caught in there, Tikey, a frog?"

"Snake," Tike said. "Serpent."

"You seem to be having quite a scuffle."

"Fight 'im day an' night."

"And he seems to be getting just a little the best of it from what I can see." She watched him from the corner of her eye.

He was a moment making his reply. He took a step forward and caught hold of her hand. She could measure the heat of his desire by the moisture in the palm of his hand. He tugged at her slow and easy and stepped backward in the path of the cow barn. "Psssst. Lady. Psst. Lady. Wanta see somethin'? Huh?"

"What are you trying to do to me? Mister?" She pulled back until she had spoken, then she gave in and walked along. "Will you please state?"

"Shh. Gonna show you somethin'."

"Something? Something what?"

"Shh. Just somethin'." It was funny to her to see him try to creep along without making any noise, when his heavy work shoes made such a grinding and a crushing sound under the soles that he could be heard all over the ranch. "Shh. C'mon."

And now, what would it be? What on the farm hadn't he already shown her, yes, in this very same way. What

would it be? Would it be a snake trying to swallow a lizard
or a lizard swallowing a frog? A nest of cliff hornets that he
had captured by plugging up the door to their nest with a
corncob? Had he dragged in some more big bones and teeth
of the prehistoric reptiles? Would he show her another rib
or a shin or a patch of skin to some mummy of a wayfar-
ing ancestor? Three flies doctoring a dead one back to life
by licking him with their tongues? Ants rubbing some lice
with their whiskers to cause them to have orgasms and to
burst out into a sweat of pure honey? A horned toad with
his belly full of red ants? Eagle feathers tied together with a
string of human skin? A red-and-white marble that he had
found? A die with no spots? Maybe just an old empty shoe
full of little baby mice. A bumblebee tied to a spool of black
thread. What? Of all the places on a six-hundred-acre farm,
why had he piled his relics so near and so close to the hay in
the cowshed?

"Tell me what it is!" She smelled the syrup odor of cattle
cake, manure, and the sweeter smell of the juicy sap in the
stems of the hay and the grass. "Tike!"

There was kind of a sad spirit about the little cowshed.
It was a magnetic electricity that was there in the stalls,
the feed boxes, the V-shaped mangers filled with dry cobs,
corn shucks, and hay. It was the radio waves of their old
memories. These waves vibrated, danced, and shone in all
the wood braces, boards, railings, props, and in the planks
and in the shingles. And the smell was not just a bittersweet
thing that came to their nostrils. No, the smells brought

with them older pictures, and the pictures carried with them the smells, the words, things done in days that some say are gone. The boards were all worn glassy slick by the hair and by the warm skin of cattle that followed crooked paths here just to know the pleasure of Tike and Ella May's hands on their tits. Still, Ella May's eyes told her a tale and a story of sad parting as she looked at the fireball sun going down and followed its rays down to where they struck against a smooth round cedar post that helped to hold up the small roof. A hot kind of grief moved in her. She sat there on a bale of hay where Tike had placed her. She felt her memories come through her. She felt a heavy weight of tired weariness come over her. Her first love of life was born in the three walls around her here. Tike had led her here to cover her with the loose hay, loose seeds, loose kisses of his own sort. They had made their separate troubles one trouble here, and all of their little stray scattered desires burned into one single light of craving here. These boards, these nails, pieces of long wire, hay, grain, and manure, all of this was one fiery match that lit the wick of their lamp. Every part and particle of the barn was a part of the one. Every single inch of it had its unknown name. And by the fire of their lamp they could see and feel around the world.

And it did seem to Ella May that her eyes strained to try to follow the rays from the sun around the world. She leaned back against a higher bale of hay and lifted her breasts in her own hands, took a deep breath, let her lips fall apart, and

wished that she could see every little hair on every little body
in the whole big wide world, like the lamp of the sun does.
Like the breath of the wind does. Like the waters wash them
all. Her wind went out and over and across and in and around
and through the whole farm, and she felt the hurts, aches,
pains, sickness, and the misery and all of the gladness of all
the things around her. And she felt the skin of her breasts
with her hands and her skin felt hot. And there was a layer
of sweat over all of her. She moved her heel up and down
inside her work shoe and felt the blistered callus rub against
the leather. She turned her feet over to the side and pushed
down hard against the straw on the dirt floor, and eased her
feet out of the shoes. She lay her head back and spread her
knees apart. The stir of the breeze felt good against her feet
and thighs.

"I cain't help it when I get to feeling this way, Lady," he
told her through her hair as he stood at her back. "I don't
know, maybe it's just because I'm a man, or something."

"Or something." She put her hand over her shoulder and
took hold of his fingers. "Did I ask you to try to help it?"

"No."

"Grandma used to tell us girls that a woman feels seven
times as much passion as a man. But I don't believe that. I
think that you feel this way every time I do, and that I feel it
every time you do. I don't know how to tell you how I feel.
I don't think any woman can tell a man how she feels. She
could talk her head off and never say it. Tike, did you take
your shirt off? Is that your skin I feel? And your overalls,

too? And your jumper? You'll take down deathly sick." She stood up and looked at him.

"Used them here for a bed." He stood before her naked and pointed down.

"You'll freeze."

"Sun's warm. Warm enough. I ain't cold. But I could stand just a little bit of your huggin' if you got some to spare."

She moved against him. He put his arms around her. She held him as she kissed the hairs on his chest and wiggled the end of her nose against his neck. The heat of their bodies soaked her dress with sweat as they stood and kissed. He kissed her eyes, ears, and her hair, the sides of her nose, and down her neck. He put his lips to her lips and she sucked his tongue. She closed her eyes and stood on tiptoe and all she felt was the tip end of his tongue pushing around against her teeth. With one hand he combed his fingers through her hair. With the other hand he rubbed the muscles of her back, shoulder blades, and squeezed her hips. They did not know how long they stood and kissed.

She felt the long hot shape of his penis pressed tight between their stomachs. As she moved her hips from side to side in a slow easy roll she felt his penis grow even warmer and longer. He touched the tip of his tongue to each of her teeth, one at a time and felt the vacant gums in two places where her teeth were out. He moved his tongue over the upper part of her mouth and as he did so he filled his mouth with saliva that she sucked into her mouth and swallowed.

They let themselves fall down onto Tike's clothes on the hay and kept their lips together for several more minutes. Tike kissed her across the shoulders and the skin of her arms. He touched his tongue to the nipples of her breasts and saw them stand up in the light of the sun. "Is little baby getting his titty milk?" she tried to tease him.

"Milk an' honey." He spoke with her left nipple between his lips. "This one's milk. This one's honey. This one's milk. This one's honey." He sucked each nipple, the right, and the left, as he talked against her skin.

"Isn't little Tikey Baby ashamed of himself to throw his mama down here on this old pile of hay just to get his dinner?" She tried to speak in a serious tone, but he held his ear against her heart, and heard her laugh under her breath. He heard a deep gurgling sound somewhere inside her, and the splashing about of waters.

"No." He used baby talk. "Itty Tikey ain'ty fwaidy."

Her stomach bounced when she laughed. He felt the muscles of her whole body jerk.

Then he spoke again. "Itty Tikey notty shamey."

"No? Mmm?"

"You got more water an' stuff splashin' aroun' inside of you than I could suck out in fifty years of hard pullin'! Quit! Shut up. Quit teasin' me!" He pushed his mouth down harder against her breast and shook his head like a bashful kid. And then he got still and quiet and asked her, " 'Smatter? 'Fraid you'll run dry? You got more joosey magoosey in these tits of yours here than any of our old milk cows."

"Tike."

"Yeah."

"Just hold me. Mmm. That's it. That's it. Be my cover. Ohhh. That's fine. Such a nice warm cover. You're just about the best blanket I ever had. Hold close, close, close. And for a long, long, long time. I just want to lay here and think. And think. And then think some more." She opened her legs and spread her knees apart while he moved and laid on her, then she closed her legs around his hips and her arms around his neck. "When you suck my nipples, Tikey, and get them all wet with your spit, and the wind blows on them, they, they, I don't know, they get real cold and hurt. This is warmer. Gooder this way."

"What you want to lay here and think about, Lady?" Tike moved his hips and penis against the hair between her legs.

"Just everything." She kissed his ear, then let her head fall back and her eyes move about the whole cowshed. "Just sort of about this whole big world so full of hard times, so full of troubles, so full of fun, with a little red fence around it."

"I wish you'd think up some kind of a way to get us a piece of nice good farmin' land, with an adobe house on it, an' a big adobe fence all around it."

"There's not but one way. And that is to just keep on working and fighting and fighting and working, and then to work and to save and to save and to fight some more," she said.

"Fight who?" he asked.

"I don't know. I'm not just positive that I know. But I think it's mainly these landlords," she told him.

"Guys that keep us in debt up to our ass all our life."

Tike moved against her an inch closer, then he moved away from her for a moment to move his right hand down to feel the hair between her legs. He squeezed and pushed and moved his fingers among the hair.

And she said, "There you go saying bad words again."

"Goshamighty, woman, you mean to say that ass is a bad word?"

"It's sure not a nicey-nice one."

"Yeah. But ever'body's got an ass. It's just your rump. Your fanny. What you're laying on right now."

Ella did not laugh, sigh, giggle, nor answer right at that moment. She laid her arms back on the hay above her head and held her eyes shut and her face to one side. She bit her bottom lip soft and easy, then her mouth fell open and her lips were damp and wide apart.

The picture of her face, her eyelids, hair, forehead, ears, cheeks, chin, was one of almost complete peace and comfort. Tike saw a trace, a tiny trace, but a trace of ache, pain, and misery there as she licked her lips and breathed. A feeling came over him. A feeling that had always come over him when he saw her look this way. It was a feeling of love, yet a feeling of fight. A love that was made out of fight, the fight that he would fight if any living human hurt or harmed or even spoke low-down or bad words about his Lady. And for a good long time he seemed to get a higher view, somehow, of their life together, their life on this gumbo land in this shack, and even the land and the shack and their cowshed he felt did not really belong to them. No. It all belonged to a man that had never set foot on it. Belonged to somebody that did not give a damn about it. Belonged to someone that didn't care about the feelings of their cowshed. Somebody somewhere that did not know the fiery seeds of words and of tears and of passions, hopes, split here on this one spot of the earth. Belonged to somebody who did not think that these people were able to think. Belonged to somebody who had their names wrote down on his money list, his sucker list. Belonged to somebody who does not know how quick we can get together and just how fast we can fight. Belongs to a man or a woman somewhere that don't even know that we're down here alive. It belongs to a disease that is the worst cancer on the face of this country, and that cancer goes hand in hand with Ku Klux, Jim Crow, and the doctrine and the gospel of race hate, and that disease is the system of slavery known as sharecropping.

Not all of this came into Tike's brain in these exact same words. No. Not all of it. A feeling came over him like one he'd had when he was a boy, and just about every day or so since then. It is the world's hardest feeling to say in words, because it is not a feeling of words alone, words only. It is an actual vision. It is a scientific fact, and all of the experts of the brain and of the mind know it very well. It is not a spirit hallucination, nor a vision based on superstition, hoodoo, voodoo, witchcraft, hocus-pocus, nor the world of heaven beyond.

It happened at all times when all Tike's hopes, wants, cravings, and troubles, accidentally or all on purpose, all came together in one solitary, single thought, usually and quite naturally his one single thought was about the person on earth that he loved most. It had been a dozen girls at the farms and the ranches around. It had come when friends and relatives from towns and from other farms brought their children out for a visit. It had happened when he was think- ing about his mother, his father, his brothers and sisters. He had had it a hundred times or more while he was going with Ella May, and he had felt it even plainer, more real, since he had been married to her. The sight of her doing her work about the place would cause him to fall into his vision. When she was away at town or at some of the neighboring farms he thought about her so plain that everything in his world came to him at the same instant. He actually saw a living thread of connection between every thought that he had ever thought, everything that had ever happened to him, and every cell in his brain, every memory, was very plainly connected up one with the other, and another with that, and so on.

The feeling was, roughly, then, that if all of these sepa- rated memories, thoughts, ideas, happenings, were all just the one Tike Hamlin, well, then, all of the things around him—house, barn, the iron water tank, the windmill, lit- tle henhouse, the old Ryckzyck shack, the whole farm, the whole ranch—they were a part of him, the same as an egg from the farm went into his mouth and down his throat and was a part of him.

Religious people, the brush arbor shouters, the holy rollers on their hay, the spiritualists in their trances, the Christian Scientists hunting for their oneness with all things, they would have given the feeling some kind of name and gone around about the country preaching the thing to others. Tike did not look at his feelings nor the ramblings of his brain, nor the work of his hands, as anything to be bought, sold, or preached or taught to others. Maybe it was a mark against him that he did not spread nor share his knowledge with the folks that had lost their hold on this feeling, but his excuse was that he just did not see nor realize nor believe that they were really lost, and he also believed that if somebody did choose to be lost, lost to their own self, lost to the world about them, then all of the hunting and searching that he could do would not help one ounce to find them.

He believed and said, "You help a hand to find a job of work that it likes to do, and that hand will find its own self."

He closed his eyes. He kissed, then sucked the tips of Ella May's ears. He kissed her left eye, then her right eye, then down along her nose, then he kissed each corner of her mouth. As he took a lungful of air into his mouth and nose, he held her bottom lip between his teeth and smelled the hay and the barn. He felt a slick juice on the fingers of his hand between her legs, and as she moved her face from side to side and her heels and toes dug into the hay, his kisses turned into little soft, easy bites that nipped her neck and her armpits, her breasts, her stomach, and her whole body.

"Know what kind of a kiss this is here, down across your belly?" he asked her.

"I can't guess," she said. "What kind?"

"Shotgun kiss."

"Why do you call it a shotgun kiss?"

"'Cause. It spreads out all over everywhere, an' it gets ever'thing in th' brush."

"Tike."

"Yes, Miss Lady."

"Isn't it about time that the little man came in out of this awful bad weather?"

"This weather bad?"

"Ohh. Mmm. It's something terrible. Just something terrible."

"Ha ha ha. Mebbe so. Mebbe so."

"Where is he?"

"Here he is. Don't you recognize 'im?"

"Ohhh. Easy. Tike. Baby. Ohhmm. Tike. Honey. Easy, Tikey."

"Hurt?"

"Teeny-weensy bit."

"Now? Lady?"

"Noooo. It's. No. It's all right now. Just don't. Push too. Too hard. Too. Fassst."

"Hurt now?"

"Huh-unh. Here. Lay down and hold me and be my

good warm blanket if you please again. And. Let's stay here a long, long, long time, what say, Tikey? You know I'm just thinking about something."

"Yeah. What?"

"Ohh. About how nice our earth house is going to be."

"Yeah. Me too. When we get it."

"Yes. When we do get it. I wonder how long it will take?" She moved under him and talked with her eyes on the shingle roof. "How long?"

"How long to build one?"

"Yes."

"I don't know. Gover'ment book tells. Where's th' book at? Didn't mess aroun' an' lose it already, did you?"

"No. It's here. Right here at my elbow. I had it stuck in my apron pocket and it fell out."

He looked at the book at her elbow. "It's fell out there, yeahh. It's okay. Ahh. It's turned to page five. Ain't no readin' on th' page. Just some pictures. One, two, three, four, five, six, seven pictures. Guys a makin' th' bricks. Gosh. Look what big ones. We could have our walls two feet thick if we just wanted to. Whew."

"Wind certainly couldn't blow any dust and dirt through a wall that thick, could it? Hmmm? Ohh. Tike, honey, baby, sweetie pie, sugar dumpling, gosh, I love you. Did you know that? Or did I ever tell you? Did I, honey, ever, ever, ever, ever, tell you how much? Gosh."

"Mixin' th' soil. Fillin' th' brick forms. Smoothin' down th' top. Takin' off th' forms. Washin' out th' forms. Layin' th' bricks out to dry. Stackin' up th' bricks to let 'em cure out good. Big stacks an' stacks of 'em with big flat boards on top. I guess that's to what? What?"

"Why, I don't know. But I would just suppose that they were covered over with boards to keep the rain from washing your bricks apart. Move closer. Move a little closer, Tikey Ikey. Is that a good name? Like it? Tikey Ikey. Tacky Wacky. Huhh?"

And he rubbed his chin against her forehead and laughed as he said, "Lissen, Miss Lady. Let me put you sorta wise to a thing or two. Just a little thing or two. Ahh. Just as long as you let me be your blanket like this, an' keep you all warm an' ever'thing like this, I don't care what name you call me by. So far, you called me some kind of a different name ever' time. So I'm a gettin' to where I just don't know what name hardly to answer to anymore."

She laughed under her breath and he felt her muscles jerk into tight knots, then get loose, and relax again. "I just call you those names to show you how much I love you, you silly old outfit."

"Yeah?"

"Yes."

"An', so now, it's Mister Wacky Ikey, or Tikey Wikey, or Woozeldy Goozeldy or somethin'. Or Mister Blanket. What'll I call you by? Miss Blanket? Nope. What? Ah. I know. I'll have to start callin' you Misses Mattress. Ha."

"Misses Mattress. Ha ha ha ha."

"Don't laugh so much."

"I'll laugh if I want to laugh. You can't stop me. Ha ha ha ha ha ha ha."

"I just don't want to fire my shot till you fire yours, Lady, I mean, Misses Blanket. But when you laugh thataway, it jerks my pecker around in your belly, and it feels so good that it makes me want to come. Lay still. I don't want to come away ahead of you, Misses Blanket. I mean, Misses Mattress."

"I will. I will, Mister Blanket. No. Not yet. It's just commencing to feel good. It'll be a few more minutes, though, before I can work myself up. Besides, Mister Blanket hadn't ought to end his fun before Misses Mattress gets hers. Tell me something to talk about. Wackioooo. Tackiooo. Ohh. About the house?"

"Our adobe house," Tike said. "Main thing's got me bested is just where, an' just how, an' just when we're a gonna get our hands on some kind of a piece of land to build it on."

"Yes. I wonder the same. It looks like we keep coming back to this same question, doesn't it?"

"Yeahmm."

"I've got an idea. And a bright one at that." Ella May's eyes looked over his shoulder. "A nice, nice, bright one. Ha. It just now came to me. Just like that."

"Like what? Spill it. Don't try to set on it like an egg an' hatch it. Spill it," he said.

"Well. First, move a little closer."

"Closer?"

"Yes. Come closer. I would like for you all, one an'

all, to please gather in just a little bit closer. I will tell you about a sure and certain way to get a piece of land to build yourselves a nice, warm, fireproof, windproof, rainproof, sweatproof, bugproof, foolproof, this proof, that proof, everything proof, nice, hot, cold, warm, cool, airtight, hidebound, cork-tipped, rubber-dipped, gold-plated, high-polished house of adobe earth. Come in just a teensy-weensy bit closer and hug me just a measly mouse warmer." The sound of her voice was like a street-corner salesman. "Come in. Just a little bit."

Tike cut her off and said, "I'm already as close as I can get. I'm pushin' just hard as I can, but think I done come to th' end of my rope. Tell your brilliant idea and quit havin' these goofy spells."

"Ohhh. But, Mister Hackey Jack, Slappy Hap, this idea is a sooper dooper one. It's positively the very best idea that has been given birth to on this ranch so far." As she spoke, she pooched her lips and moved her body.

"Give birth to it, then, an' f'r Jesus' sakes, don't keep me so much in suspenders," he said.

"Wellll. Here it is. Get ready."

"I been ready to come for ten minutes," he said.

"Hold your horses. I'll be right with you. Now. You want to hear the bright idea? Sure?"

"Whattaya think I'm a-layin' here a-waitin' on? Th' new mornin' train?" he said.

And she said, "Well. Then. Here it is. Here it is for certain this time."

"Shoot."

"Don't you dare shoot. Not yet."

"Tell it!"

"Well, the very next time that one of those big mean old dust storms comes along, why, you wait till it gets just at its worst, see? Then."

"Then."

"Then you grab your hat and run out and catch it."

"Yeeeehh."

"Then. You put your hand over your hat, like this." She slapped him in the middle of the back. "Like, so."

"So ho ho ho." He acted like he was coughing. "What?"

"Then you run over to the iron water tank, and you stick the hat and all, dust storm and all, down under the water, and you hold it down there till it tames down, and all of the wind and air goes out of it, and it just turns into soil, dirt again. Then you go and you lay it down somewhere, anywhere you want to, and it will be your land. Your farm. Your ranch."

And Tike told her, "By grabs an' by grasshoppers, I'm a-gonna do that. That very thing. I swear by twenty rows of burnt corn, I'll do it. I'll do it just as sure as I'm a layin' here."

"Will you, sure enough? Tike?" She opened her eyes wide and spoke in the manner of a fairy poet beholding the folding and the unfolding of a homeless flower. "Will you, ohhh, will you really? Really? Will yooo? Ohhh. Deah. My deah. You don't know, you just don't know, you never will know, how it would thrill me, and fill me, and chill me and frill me and dill me and spill me and drill me and lil me and hill me and till me and bill me and jack me and jill me. You just don't have any idea, any ideeeaa, my dyeahhh, to see you really do something, anything, anything, just so it was something, anything. Ohh. Ahhmm. Tikus. My little Mikus."

"My little tokus," he said. "You sound like one of them screwballs that lives on millionaire hill. You ain't been out sleepin' with none of them bats, have you?"

"Oooo. Nooo."

"Hush yer trap, then."

"One has to talk, doesn't one?"

"Yeah . . . But one's goddang jaw hadn't oughta run plumb off with one. Had one?"

"You've injured my self-esteem. You've dealt a blow, and a sorry blow, to my pride. You've insulted my creative soul. And I refuse to speak to you any longahhh. You have squelched my career. Good-bye. Ohhh!"

Tike did not make any sort of a reply right then. He lifted his face above hers and whistled a little tune. And then when his little tune was whistled out, there was no sound in the barn nor in the hay, except outside there jumped and buzzed a few grasshoppers that had managed to stay alive so late in the summer.

Together they moved, rolled, hugged onto one another on the overalls and jumper and on the lightweight cotton dress.

And after a few more minutes had gone by with no more than the sound of their breath, their kisses, their nips, bites, and grunts, Tike asked her, "Lady. How does it feel? Say."

"Good."

"Just good?"

"Just good."

"I always like to hear you tell me how it feels."

"Just goody, good, good."

"I mean, ah, my penis, Lady. How does it feel when it's way up inside your belly thisaway? Huh?" He raised himself up on his hands to see the hair on their stomachs wet and stuck together with the juices and the liquids that flowed from her. "All, all, all th' way in. All, all, all, th' way in. Want me to hold it in a lot longer, Lady? Gosh. I want to do what you want me to do. I can hold it in you all day if you like it thataway."

"Teeny more."

"How's it feel? I ask'd you."

"How?"

"Yeah."

"I don't know."

"Does it feel big?"

"Uh-huh."

"What else?"

"Hot. Big. Slick. Juicy. Close."

"What else?"

"Everything. Come on. Hold me tight. Kiss me. Ohh-hhmmm. Tike. Close. Here. Kiss. Oh. Oh. Ohhh. Squeeze me tight. Tighter. Tight as you can. And don't talk any more."

"Comin', Lady?"

She shook her head yes.

"Good. Goood. Come. Come real, real, real good. Let your whole self go. Lady. Gosh. Lady."

"Kiss me. Long time. Don't talk."

Back and forth, side to side, they moved on their bed on the hay. Back and forth, side to side, they moved their hips, their feet, their legs, their whole bodies. Their arms tied into knots like vines climbing trees, and the trees moved and swayed, and there was a time and a rhythm to the blend of the movement. And inside the door of her womb she felt her inner organs and tissues, all her muscles and glands, felt them roll, squeeze, squeeze, and roll, and felt that every inch of her whole being stretched, reached, felt out, felt in, felt all around the shape of his penis. So magnified and so keen were her feelings that her inner nerves could even feel the bumps, the ridges, the pimples, the few stray hairs along the shaft of his male rod. And inwardly she caressed, touched, petted, and fondled, squeezed, the whole length and all of the sides of the penis. And this caused her to work and to move and to roll and to breathe hard, to forget her name, her own self completely. She felt her organs fondle, and she felt them squeeze, suck, gently, easily, softly, smoothly, wet, damp, slick, and there was a fire, a heat, a heat that was his, a heat that was only his, and a fire all in her that was his fire, and only his fire, and the heat was him, the fire was in his blood, the heat, that juicy, oily, stiff hard flesh that was him. The motion of her hips caused the lips of her hole and her passage to suck, suck, suck, suck. And such a feeling, such a fire, such a blaze of warmth and life as she felt her belly suck with all her strength, all her power, suck, suck, suck, with all her blood, all her heat, all her life. As he moved against her to hold it in a hundredth of an inch closer, it felt in her stomach that he had come a hundred miles closer to her. The penis jumped, jerked, and moved up and down against her insides as he started to come. And as the drops of his juice came from the end of his penis, each drop sent her into rolls, squirms, fits, convulsions of a kind past either pain or joy. Every drop that struck against her nerves caused her to feel such a fit of fire and freedom as she could never say in words, nor even imagine in her wildest and hottest dreams. She only desired that her insides suck each and every drop, each and every drop, of this hot juice that shot from his stomach. Her feeling was that as she fondled, stroked, and touched her inner organs against his heat and mixed her own inner juices with his new hot blood, somehow, in an inner way, in a big inner and outer way, all of the scattered troubles, hopes, fears, hurts of her whole existence were following a path, a route, or a way of some one bigger purpose, and in her mind she saw the fires of that higher thing and the way and the path to it, and saw the one big answer to every problem, every question that had ever dealt her pain. It felt like he was her and she was him, and he was in her and she was in him, and that he was all about her while she was at the same time all about him. The feeling was a vision and the vision showed the way out. And as she sucked the last drops of his blood and his seed into the folds of her innermost soul and self, she felt her whole body lift, pull, squeeze, then lift again, tremble, shake, and quiver, and in her fires of her stomach she strained and moved to bathe his blood into the rumble and the thunder of her own. And then she felt the feelings rise so high and so strong that her body melted into a single note of music to the sky and when the blaze of his heat met with the fires of her fire, then there was such a bright lightness in them both that neither of their senses could feel it, neither of their eyes could face it.

He had held her all of the time that she had moved and rolled and come to her orgasm on his clothes on the hay. He had felt her womb milk his penis, and his feelings had been to him exactly as they had been to her. He was learning a little at a time how to stay until she had come and till she became quiet and still in the few minutes after it. He kept his penis in her even after he had shot all of his juice into her belly. He spent several minutes doing this because she had acted nervous several times when he jumped up and left her. A thousand and one things came back into his mind, things that he ought to be doing, working at, fixing up, getting ready for. His brain commenced to show up moving pictures of all of the jobs he had started, the ones that he had finished, and the ones that had to be started right away. This. That. And the other thing. This, that, and something else. All of this work, all of these jobs, all of this sweat and good labor poured into a useless bucket and down a senseless drain on a piece of land that did not belong to him, did not shelter Ella May, did not keep them away from the germs, the filth, the misery, did not keep their hides from the heat nor the cold, did not look good to their eyes, and by the law of the land they could not lift a hand to build the place into that nicer one because the man that owned it did not care about all of this. Oh. These. These things. And then a lot of other things came and went, roared and buzzed around in his brain. He tried to dream up some earthly scheme to get his hands on a piece of good farmland to raise up that house of earth on. Ohh. Yes. That Department of Agriculture book was an awful mighty good thing, laying there at her elbow on that hay. But it made their biggest misery even bigger, and their biggest dream even plainer, and their biggest craving ten times more to be craved. A fireproof, windproof, dirtproof, bugproof, thief-proof house of earth. His penis had become limber, and her moving had forced it out of her hole.

He felt the liquids from her womb smeared through the hairs on his stomach, between his legs, over his balls, and felt the end of his penis as it moved limber on the hay and was covered with lint, dust, and fine splinters of straw. After a few minutes of thinking, figuring, picturing, and puzzling out his problem about the house and the piece of land, the lint and the straw commenced to dry in the air and to cause him to itch and hurt.

He stood up with Ella May and they leaned against one another for a few moments to get their wits together again, and to add up their new thoughts. Their arms bent around each other. They stood without talking. Only a few whispered words passed between their lips, and these were mumbled, stuttered, spoken in ways that meant nothing, each one talking, whispering to his self. A little of nothing and a touch of everything.

A half an hour after that they were back by the same little bench where they had lifted the cream cans three hours before. A pan of hot soapy water threw its steam in the air as Ella May stood and held her dress above her stomach to wash between her legs with a rag. Tike said curse words about the splinters of hay and straw that had dried and stuck on the hairs and the skin of his stomach, crotch, and legs. "Wonder what it'd be like for me to put this in you with alla these straws an' stickers on it? Lady?" he asked her as they both washed. "Huhhh?"

"There goes that old evil mouth of yours again, Tike Hamlin."

"Just crost my mind," he said.

"If the shadow of a hungry boll weevil was to cross that brain of yours, it would blot your thoughts out for the next ten years. Hush up."

"No. I'm really a awful deep-thinkin' man, Ella."

"About as deep as the dirt under your fingernails. Which is pretty deep, at that, I suppose." She dropped her dress down into place again, wrung her rag out several times in the pan, and hid both the pan and the rags back in under the floor. "Did you put your rag in the pan, Tike?"

"Naww. I tossed it up on toppa th' house. I figured it might help to hold some of them shingles from takin' off so fast," he said as he moved up and down on his toes and fastened the clips of his overall suspenders over their metal buttons. "Goshamighty. You know I feel just like a new man. Feel like I'm all good an' set to go to worryin' myself crazy again. You know, Lady, they said that the Good Lord run Adam an' Eve outta th' garden of Paradise 'cause they done what we just got through doin'."

"And so? What has Adam and Eve got to do with us out here on this dried-up and blown-away wheat farm living like a couple of Egypt's slaves?"

"I'm just about to decide that th' Lord was dead wrong about what he done to poor old Adam an' Eve. I'm just a-rollin' it over in my mind. But, you know, I swear to God an' little channel cats, Honey, th' more we do that, th' closer to heaven I get. Of course, now, that was a mighty long time back, back when God chased 'em out. I just wonder. You reckon it felt as good an' tasted as good then as it does nowadays?"

"I'm positive that you will just have to go up there in the roost and get down on your hands and knees and ask God himself about that. I wouldn't know, I'm sure," she said. "If it's like this old house here, it has gotten worse, instead of better, since the year of One."

"Could be that the houses has got worse. But I'm fairly sure that th' juicin's got lots better." There was a slow, joking drawl in his speech. "Say. Lady. It's a good thing that you dropped your dress down just when you did. Know it?"

"What's grazing through your vulgar mind now? Mister Hamlin?" As she talked to him, she walked up and down the yard, taking an armful of clothes off the line. She felt of a dish towel that hung on a nail on the wall to see if it had dried since she put it there. "Pray tell?"

"I could see old Grampaw Hamlin's old eyes just a firin' and a blazin' all of th' way from his front porch over acrost th' field, an' then acrost th' road, an' then away up over th' mailbox, an' right on up acrost that fence, an' right up to where you was a standin' there with your dress all snatched up." Tike took a seat on the old cellar door that slanted from the ground up to the top of its low pile of dirt that covered the cellar over. "Yes sir. I could see his old eyes just a blazin' blue dynamite."

"I will certainly look forward to the day when something takes place around this country which will cause your mind to think above your belly. I'm not at all certain just what sort of an event could bring that about, but something has got to, before you run yourself completely screw loose on the subject of naked skin. As far as old Grandpa Hamlin is concerned, and his old eyes seeing my naked rear all the way across his farm and that road and our farm, well, I'm not the least ounce worried. He has stood in the breeze over yonder and washed his legs and his belly clean just as much, just as often, maybe a lot oftener, than we ever did. So what does that add up to? Pooh." She walked to the west screen door and tossed her armful of clothes in onto the seat of a chair.

"Adds up to Grampaw a pretty clean old crotch, I reckon." Tike spit down onto the ground and watched it roll up into a small dusty ball. "Must be clean. I cain't smell it from over here. Can you?"

"No." The screen slammed shut with a rattle that shook the entire house. "Dern it. I keep forgetting that you put that big tight spring on that door. I jerks the thing shut so hard I fear that the whole edifice will just collapse." As she said the last word, *collapse*, she made a rolling motion of her arms in the air.

"Don't talk so loud. You'll shake th' damn shack down." Tike laughed as he picked at his warty hand and wiped the blood down against the rotten cellar door. "Take it easy."

"You're certainly taking it easy over there. You don't ever let yourself get mad enough to pitch in and do some hard honest work, do you?" She held her hands on her hips as she walked past him to put her clothesline pole back in its place. "I'd sure like to see something come along that would just rouse you up right good and fighting mad. I'd get some work out of you then."

And Tike smeared wart blood down across his thumb and said, "I ain't no fighter, Lady, I'm a hay layer."

"If you don't jump yourself a rabbit from up there and help me to do this work, you never will roll in any of your old hay with me for your mattress anymore."

"Sounds threatenin'." He leaned on his elbow and blinked his eyes across the pasture to the west.

"What was that two-dollar crack?" She stood at his side with her fists doubled up. "Mister?"

"I was just remarkin' that this here weather looks awful threatenin'. Threatenin'." He raised up his arms to guard his face as though he expected her to slap his ears.

"I know you like a book, Tike Hamlin. You think that I am just kidding with you? You just wait till tonight. In bed."

"You ain't got nothing I'd want in my bed."

"You? What? Allll right, sir, mister, just allll right for you. You just wait till night comes. I know you better than you know your own self. I know just exactly what you will say. I already know it. I don't even have to use my brain to know you better than I know my own name. I can read your old empty head a whole lot easier than I can read a first-grade reader."

"I got a hell of a lot pertier gal than you that I meet ever' day right there in that cowshed. I was down there with 'er less than an hour ago. You cain't threaten me with your dang old wore-out threats. Git. Beat it. Go peddle your manure." He raised up and stood on his feet at her back.

"Of all the men that I could have married. And to think that I had to pick you out of them all." She shook her head and turned away from him as he made a step to stand in front of her. Each step that he took, she turned away. He was always at her back. She would not look him in the face. She acted like she was madder than she really was. "I picked you. You."

Tike put his arms around her and held the nipples of her breasts again in the palms of his hands. He bit the skin of her neck from behind as he hugged her close and said, "Yeahh. Gee. Just think, Hon. If you'd a-married somebody else 'sides me, you coulda had a whole six hundred an' forty acres of th' best land in this whole country with a cement house an' all a th' fancy trimmin's on it. Like your paw wanted. I many times just stand an' wonder, wonder why you're a-standin' here by this ole rotting pile of nothin' with me fer a husban'. Know?"

"I'm standing right here, here. Here. Simply just because I am not standing anywhere else! You silly idiot! You are my husband because I gave that old clerk two dollars and a half of our hard-earned money to marry us! And I'm standing here looking at this old rotten fell-down house because, well, because it's just about the funniest and the most miserable little old thing that I ever did lay my two eyes on! It's lots funnier to me than those old funny papers I'm pasting up on the walls inside! And as for my old rich moneybags daddy, well, he can just pass out his farms and his good houses to the rest of his young'uns that will kneel down in front of him and do what he says. He'll do their thinking, and their eating, and their breathing, and their sleeping for them for all of the rest of the days of their lives, and he'll find their right mate for them and go to bed for them and open up their legs for them and show them everything. And, and, and. Oh. Well. Shut up. That is a silly question to ask a body anyhow. What I'm mainly wondering is about me and you, us, Tike. How much longer are we going to be caught here in this old jail, anyway?" Her lips touched his arm that was around her.

The sun against the south wall by them was warm, and a cream can made a loud noise expanding in the heat. Thirsty cattle bawled on their trail to the barn. A hen and a rooster rustled under the floor. Several hogs grunted and wallowed in their cool places under the house also. A vibration was set up in the air that shook the wall and caused a thimbleful of powdery rosin, rotten wood dust, to sift from under a window board and down on top of an iron cream can. They gritted their teeth in a look of quick and deathly hate as the sound of the falling wood dust struck their ears. Their lips were so tight against their teeth that no living blood could flow, and in the last few rays of the sundown their faces took on a look of pale, fighting bitterness.

II

TERMITES

Ella May started to walk into the house. She held her head down, and pulled Tike along by his hand. She saw loose feathers, fine, whipped straw and grass seeds, wheat hulls, and low dust blow under their feet. She smiled and he smiled. On each face it was a smile that covered up a hurt. The whole farm had a move on today, and as they walked, so slowly, they had to pick out their steps ahead of them, thinking. The house moved along in their eyes as they kept their heads down. It was a bright day. Yes. Away to the north, across the 66 Highway a mile away, on out across Ben Lomond's hog pastures, on for several miles over the black gumbo wheat lands, on to the north toward the upper north plains, away on to the smoky horizon of the carbon black plants, over and above all of this were the blue sky and light clouds of a pretty day. And down to the south, over wheat lands as flat as a floor, as level as a yardstick, and to the Cap Rock cliffs that fell down into the sandy cotton farms around Clarendon, it was a clear day.

Tike and Ella May had ridden the fast bareback ponies

all up and down the Cap Rock cliffs a hundred, a thousand times. They had gone out on foot and walked the hot
and the cold miles in every sort of weather, up, down, in,
over, under, and across the canyons, washes, ditches, gullies. Holding hands together, they had kicked their feet and
skinned their shoes against the flat sandrocks, round flints,
and against the roots and trunks of the ironwood bushes,
the ironweeds, and the several dozen kinds of cactus and
stickers that carry daggers and thorns tipped and dipped
in nature's stinging poison. Together they had held their
hands against their ears and felt the high wind pull at their
hair as the fast-rolling tumbleweeds bounced and jumped
out across the flats and they had yelled, "Look at that old
tumbleweed! Watch 'er go! Watch it! Watch it roll and jump
off from that cliff!"

And the tumbleweeds always lit somewhere down below, somewhere down "on some cotton farmer's place," as
Tike put it. "When old mama nature wants to sweep our
good old upper plains off real good and clean, she always
uses those lower plains as a place to sweep her trash in!"

And Ella May would laugh. She always laughed. She
laughed in a way that was easy for her. She laughed best,
most times, when the crops, the winds, the debts, the worries, the fears and doubts of the world, splashed their highest. This laugh was not a laugh that made fun of a slim lady
for being slim, a fat lady for being fat, or an ugly person
for being ugly, it was not a laugh of this kind, not of the
kind that makes fun of you because you are you. It came

across her face, in her throat, from her stomach, her whole body at the same time, and she had a way of doing it in such an easy manner that the whole country just called it "Ella May's laugh." Other ones tried to add a little bit onto it, and said, "There's that Ella May flying in the wind again." "Ella May's ticklebox has blowed over." "Things must be pretty tough over at her house, she's laughing again." As a little girl, she had used her voice to make herself heard in the face and teeth of high hard winds, sand, gravel, straw, papers, all sorts of dry, brittle, noisy things that fill the air with loud sounds as they get taken into the winds of the plains. More than any kind of a laugh, it was a way that she had of raising, lifting her voice, and saying, "Whooooo," or "Wheeee," or "Tiiiikkkee!" Or "Graaannn'paw!" Or "Looookkkyy!" She always shouted out this first word, whatever it was, that she was thinking about, or if she was working all alone with the livestock, chickens, or the tractor, or the harvesting, and then the laugh came, after that, she would all at once remember that other people had heard her, and like she was, in a way, and in the same breath, making a little bit of fun of her own self, and all of her earthly sorrows in one breath. People for a mile on the windward side of her could hear her on her first few words and they strained their ears to hear what was coming next, but naturally they couldn't catch what it was.

As they walked up to the front door on the east, Tike's eyes fell down across the top of the old flat sandstone that had been carried up from the canyons. He laughed in his way. A way that was very different from Ella May's. His throat simply filled with a low kind of chuckle that echoed all through his lungs and body. He always laughed soft as the lint on the straw, quiet as the skin on the new moon, easier than Ella May, and never as loud, unless he was shouting at her across the yard, or at a friend in town across one of the streets. His face came to life and showed his whole life on it as he laughed, but he just seemed to be laughing inside his own self right back at his own misery. He looked down at the old flat stone steps, the old sandy rock, and said, "And this, Elly, ah, this is, I guess, what you can call our first stepstone to something real."

She put one foot on the top of the rock and stepped up into the door, and grunted, "Whew. I hope that something we do is a stepping stone to something real." Her eyes had a young, fiery wildness in them as they looked around the room in hate. The sound of her teeth gritting together came to Tike's ear as he walked in behind her.

"Not very much to look at, is it?" was all that he could say as he fell down on his stomach across their bed. It seemed to his nose that the powdery cloud of dust came up out of the patchwork quilt. He made a snorting sound with his lips and nose.

And Ella May had already learned long before now what was in the thoughts of Tike Hamlin every time that his mouth and nose made this nervous snorting sound. He was mad. Sore. He was getting fed up and disgusted with the whole thing. Tike Hamlin was a man to fight, and she knew that this snort of his meant that he was mad enough, angry enough, and nervous enough to fight. Her brain boiled as she thought:

"But. Fight what? Fight who? Fight where? When? The wind, or the rain? Fight the moon and the stars? Rip off his clothes and fight the seasons and the clouds? Fight the wind and fight the dust because it came at the wrong time, never at the right time? Fight the Sixty-Six Highway over yonder because it ran in the wrong directions? Go and fight everybody at the Star Route school? Fight all of the neighbors around? Fight the hogs and dogs, chickens, for loafing around under the house? Fight the rooster for chasing after the hen? Fight the old boar hog because he chased and rooted and bit the little baby pigs? Fight the turkey hen because she flew too high up on top of the windmill platform and then screamed like an idiot till she nearly drove the whole farm crazy? Fight what? Fight who? When? Where? Fight the people that come out across the yard to collect all kinds of silly debts? Go fight the state capitol, the city hall, the public toilet? What?" It was all of this. It was more than this. It was something that was so big that it was hard for words to say, and it was something that was mixed up and messed up in every little job that their fingers touched upon, each little step their feet had to take, something that was a burning pain in every chore and every job around the farm, something, something, it was something so little, so little, that it was in everything they went about. And it was just because Tike was filled with all these feelings that Ella May almost smiled when he snorted a few more times. She lifted her face up toward the ceiling as she slipped her dress up over her head, and laid it down over the back of a cane-bottom chair. In her nose she felt the burn, the little burn, that faraway, dim and distant little burn that the dust from the house had always caused her. She took a deep breath. She felt her tears washing away all of the eye pencil out of her eyebrows. She tried to wipe these away to hide them from Tike on the bed, but the ends of her fingers only smeared the eye shadow on her cheeks, and made her look hollow-cheeked, skinny, scary, something like the shadow on a dried skull just at sundown in the colors.

"Elly." Tike pushed his nose and mouth down hard against the bedclothes. "Hon."

"What?" she answered him with her back turned. She kicked her shoes off as easily as she could without disturbing what Tike was about to say. "Huh?"

"Somethin' I got to tell. Eatin' my whole guts out. I got to tell it, tell it, even if you kill me for it. Even if you take up a chopping axe and run me clean off of the place." His hands clawed into the covers on the mattress and the springs squeaked like a canary bird caught in a corner. "I'm going nuts. Bats. Just can't keep it to myself no longer."

Ella put her arms and head through the collar of a clean blue cotton dress with round white dots all over it, and as she pulled the cloth down at the bottom and buttoned two buttons at her waist, she answered, "We never did make a practice of keeping things a secret from one another, did we, Mister?"

"No, but."

"But what? Sir?"

"This is bad. Mean. Something as big as all of our other worries put together. Something that's bigger than that, even." Tike pounded the bed with the palm of his hand, and pulled at his hair with his other five fingers. "Even worse than all of them."

Ella stood and looked at the wallpaper, its cracks, rips, dust, and cobwebs that no earthly woman could ever clean or hope to clean as fast as they came along. Her back was still turned to Tike. "Yes . . . ?"

"You know, you remember last year."

"Yes. What about last year?"

"Well. Last year we rented this six hundred acres, didn't we?"

"Yes . . ."

"And we paid down the cash money for it, didn't we?" A hot kind of torture made him sound like he was badly embarrassed.

"Yes." Her voice rasped, barely above a dry whisper. She felt the dust, dirt, filth, of the whole house in her mouth as she rubbed her face with both hands and swayed on her feet.

"Hon. It's not me, my own self, that I'm worried about, or even thinking about. It's not me. I have always seen the hard side, and lived on the dirty side, and the rotten side of things; but you've not. You've not ever been any lower down than to be the daughter of a big man that owns lots of land and lots of farms, and you've always lived in a big stone twelve-room house, and had at least a few of the good things in this old world. You're used to them. Your mind and your plans and your thoughts and your hopes, everything about you has always been, well, sort of, sort of way up the ladder above me. I remember how I wanted to be a big man like your dad all my life, and how I itched and craved and burned inside me to be a big owner, or a big man, a big manager, a foreman, a boss of some kind, some kind or another over a big stretch of land just as far in every direction as my eyes could see. But I never was anything, nothing more than just the old hardworking son of, well, a family of folks that lost their land to your very father, that was several years ago."

"And? What about right now? Listen! Mister Tike Hamlin!" She turned around and stamped her feet down against the floor and yelled out in a fit of temper, "If you're going to start throwing my old rich daddy at me anymore, I'm just going to walk right out that door and I'll stay gone! I'm not going to stand here every day of my life and hear no man of mine whimper and moan and pull all of his hair out and weep both of his eyes out just because I happen to have a father that owns a lot of farms! Yes! He used every trick of money to get your folks' farm away from them! Just like he used those same tricks to get a dozen other people off their farms! Or to make renters out of them! I already know all of this side of my life ten thousand times better than you, Tike Hamlin, ever will or ever could, even if you beat your brains smack out against that windmill yonder, or this bedpost here every day of your life! For the next thousand years! I kept his books and his dollars and his pennies and his debts and his interests and his mortgages, every nickel, every rotten cent of it, in and out, in and out, for six of the best years of my life! Don't you lay there like a baby and cry to me about my old rich daddy! Don't try to tell me where I ought to live! Nor how! Nor anything more about it! For God's sake! For Christ's sake! For my sake and for your sake! Tike. You say one more word about me and my family busting up, and I swear to you that I'll walk right out that door there! And you'll never see hide nor hair of me in your whole life again!" Her voice broke into a hot, broken scream as she swung her hands in the room, and she breathed hard to try to keep from crying. "God!" She held both of her hands flat against the wallpaper and held her wet cheek against her knuckles as she felt her eyebrow shadow run worse than ever.

Tike had quieted down a bit. He spoke a bit softer, and his words had the sound of coming through a pile of cotton. "It's bad to be a dirt renter. Low as we could ever fall."

"Well, then, if that's all that you have ever been, how is it that you fume and fuss and fret all over the place now, trying to tell me how far you fell?" She kept on holding her face against her hands, and her eyes looked out the north window. There was the light of a sad reflection in her eyes.

"I fell."

"How on earth could you? You're a renter now. You have always been one. All of your born days. Where did you fall to? Why all of this falling business all of a sudden?" Her crying tears left the dark stains of her cheeks on the backs of her hands.

"Old Banker Woodridge wouldn't rent us this farm for another year."

Ella let her body slide down the wall and onto the floor. She sat with her feet crossed under her dress and blinked her eyes. "No? When did you see old man Woodridge? You didn't let me know. I didn't know that our year was up yet."

He licked the heat of his lips against the quilt. "Up last week."

She felt weak, nervous, shaky inside. She felt even too dizzy to answer Tike just then. She looked at her stack of old papers and her dishpan of flour paste.

And he said once more, to the wall behind his bed, "Yeahhp. Up last week. I dropped into his office and tried to rent for one more year. He shook his head. No soap. No dice. Nothing doing."

"Soooooo?"

Tike squeezed his two hands into his hair so tight and so hard the pain brought tears into his own eyes. "So. Ah. Well. That's just what I was trying to tell you."

"Soooo. We move, huh?" She sucked her upper lip and looked downward at her lap.

"No. Not moving."

"Not moving."

"Huh-uh."

"Nor not renting again, either one?"

And Tike said, "Huh-uh."

She felt the wall touch hard against the back of her head as she leaned back, folded her hands down in her lap, and asked through her teardrops, "Not renting? Not leaving? Not this? Not that? Well, my kind friend"—her words came as slow as new tears—"maybe you could make yourself just a little bit plainer. Just what, then, are we doing?"

"Glad you said, 'we.' " Tike smiled to himself. "I think I like the sound of that word better than any other one that I ever heard anybody say." He closed his eyes shut and said upward to the wall, "We."

"We. What?" She didn't move.

"We're ten times worse than renters. Hon."

"How?"

"Just are. Oh. Know why he wouldn't let us have the place on rent for cash another year?" Tike ground his teeth together.

"Why not?"

"Says he's about to build a new house on it. Don't want to rent it out for no whole year at a time. He might even want to move out here and farm his six hundred and live here his own self. Says if it's rented out for a whole year at a time, he could never put him up no new house on it."

"Soooo?"

Tike rubbed his mouth with the back of his hand, and felt his days-old beard stick to his fingers. "So. Well. He said that the only way he'd let us live on it was, ahh, on the shares."

That word *shares* struck a dumb, sour, shaky chord in the brain and in the thoughts of Ella May Hamlin. Her tongue was sticky, covered with a gummy, gluey, sickly spit that flooded her throat and kept her from speaking right at that minute. A tight, twisted pain exploded on her face, and the blood veins in her neck and arms stood up like roots as she finally fought to say, in a beaten, whipped, lost whisper, "Shares?"

Tike got up from the bed and stood with his hands covering both of his eyes. He staggered on his two feet on the floor. He chewed his lips until they were wet, then till they turned a blue, black, purple, and then he snorted again in his paralyzed, insane, mad, and drunken way, and walked up and down the floor, only two or three feet from the hem of Ella's cotton dress, covered with little white dots. He made a coughing sound as he cleared out his throat, and talked mostly to the winds:

"A farmer is good. It's as good a job as a man can do. Good as any man or any woman in the whole world can do. It's good because it's good and a man can be good. He can do good and he can feel like he's doing some good. And a farmer. Well, a farmer is good. But then you take a farmer that messes around and gets in debt to some outfit, and then he hits a hard row or two, and some rough and rocky country, or bad winds, or hot times, or dry spells, or washouts, floods, cloudbursts, or like that, and he loses what he's got a hold of. And then, well, then he falls down, and he gets to be a renter off of somebody else. He's lost what was a part of his skin and his bones and his heart and his soul, and so his mind and his fighting's not on his farm no more, not on it no more like it was before. Not on it. Because he's just a-renting now. He's not no owner now. Just a renter. And then, for God's sake, how low down the ladder is he? My good God. He's down just about as low and as lousy as he'll ever get, or as he thinks that he'll ever get. I felt that way. I had some care and some plans and some pep and some piss and some vinegar about me when I used to work on my own folks' place, but then since I fell down to just being a renter, I don't know, I don't know why, I never will know why, but I sort of seemed to lose about half of that old stuff that I had in me, felt in me toward my land and my seeds and my seasons. And then I went and I fell down ten times lower and lower than to be even a renter! For God's sake in heaven! Elly! Elly! Hon! I've lost all of my hold on my whole world! I've messed around and let myself fall so low, so damned low, as to end up being just another cropper! Cropping on the shares!" And for a full half minute Tike stood still, listening for Ella to say something, as he looked out the east door toward the cow barn.

Ella May felt a sour belch come from her stomach up into her nostrils, and muddy little tears caused her eyes to shine through the room. She closed her eyes and saw jerks and kinks of her whole life in her mind and in the room. She laid her head back against the wallpaper again and smelled the rot and the filth of the place. Exactly one mile out the window and to the north she saw two cars running past on the 66. Her face felt like a cake of mud to her when she smiled. "Look at those two cars."

"Uh-huh." Tike leaned the back of his head against the door frame. "One runs like a giant. One runs like a dwarf. One runs like a Cadillac, and th' other'n like an Austin."

"Little bitty one looks like some kind of a little teeny-bitsy termite or a bug of some kind. Don't it?" Ella's tears tasted salty and gritty on her tongue and lips, and a vacant, gummy, far-off feeling was in her words. "Termites. Ha ha ha."

Tike kept his hands in his hip pockets, his thumbs stuck out. He tapped his left shoe heel against the worm-eaten floor, and with his right shoe he kicked against the edge of a thin, hard, long-gone rim of cheap linoleum. Ella tried to smile. He smiled away toward the highway, over the fences and the fields, over all of the rot and troubles. And he spoke: "Termites. Ha." And his voice had a wide-open flat tone. And his face smiled with the smile that had made him ten thousand friends and enemies in his thirty-three years.

His face smiled. His face smiled with all of the puzzles, the echoes, the visions of every man that followed the plow and the seed and the seasons. His eyes were marbles and they reflected, like radio, like television, all of the earth rays of sorrow. He bent his knees and started to sit down in the doorway, but thought it would make Ella May feel better if he stood up. He made his body stand up tall and straight as he could, then rested his head against the door frame. His eyes looked away through the wind and watched the large car and the small one fade out down the road to the west. His shoes kicked more loose hunks of linoleum off the edge, and he gripped his hands so tight inside his pockets that his fingernails made deep purplish gashes in the palms of his hands.

His face smiled in the same old wind that he had felt, smelled, and known as a thing of life or death all of his life there. The wind was a thing of the weather, and the weather was the life or the death of people and crops. He had always sort of halfway frowned, halfway smiled, into the weather, up into the sun, up to the stars that chase around the big blue bowl. Blue northern blizzards cut grass blades. The noses and ears of all of his animals were frostbitten. Tike had learned to square, to squint, to wrinkle his face up as he walked into the whistling winds of the cold seasons. The right hot fiery sun of the hot spells, its dusts, its sweat, its jumping and dancing heat, he had learned to smile into that, too. And the rain. The wild and senseless, loose, washing, and running rains the same. All of these things had carved, shaped, and polished down his fore-head. All of these were on his face, in his squint, were a part of that friendly smile for his people, or that storming sneer of hate that came over him as he talked words about his enemies and the folks that had dealt him hurt. And his sneer, his scowl, his snarl, even his squint, his smile, they all came over him a hundred times a day, and a thousand, and sometimes all of these looks came over his face and these feelings ran through his blood a hundred times, all of them from his hate, to his squint, to his smile, to his laugh, in just one single solitary minute.

"Ella, hon," he asked her, "just what does folks mean when they say, 'Termite,' anyhow?"

"Termite?" Ella's neck stretched as she took a last look at the two cars through the rusted window screen and the half-open window. "A termite?" She rested her chin on the window ledge.

"Yeah."

"It's a little bitty bug, or some kind of a little teeny worm, or a little spider, or something like that." The rust from the screen caused her to sniff. "Like that, I guess."

"What's he do for a livin'?"

"I don't know. Don't ask me so many silly things. What do you think I am, your walking bookshelf?" She rubbed her hand on a muscle above her knee and felt the heat of her hand against her skin. She had a pout on her face that told Tike that he should not waste his life away looking out across the pasture to the highway when there were warmer things and closer things. She hoped that he would see the black-and-blue bruised spot on her muscle, and each minute that he looked the other direction caused her to ache and feel lonesome inside herself. She rubbed her thigh faster and harder and slowly moved her hand higher up on her leg so that the bruised spot could be seen easier. For a few moments Tike did not seem to pay her any mind. She felt several lonely years of the winds of the plains blow through her as she said, "Silly."

"Schoolteacher, ain't you?" He looked east and saw several of his milk cows standing around the barn, anxious to be milked. "You yap half of your life away tryin' to knock some sense into them thick skull kids at that old Star Route school. But now I ask you what a little bug is, I mean, what a termite is, an' you just set there an' tell me I'm silly."

"You are silly. Silly. That's what you are." She rubbed her bruise still harder. "Old Mister Silly. Old Silly Mister Tike Hamlin. He doesn't know if he's going or if he's coming."

Tike turned around and looked at her. She leaned back harder against the wall and her mouth opened as she let her eyes look down at her rubbing hand. Tike felt a distant rumbling and a hot trembling come over him as he told her, "Tell me what a termite is. I'm not goin' to ask you no more."

"Old Tikey. He don't know. He doesn't know if he's going or coming."

"I'll be coming if you don't stop rubbing your leg that way and pull your dress down. Lord's little puppy dogs, Honey, how much heat do you think I can take an' not bust a gut?" He turned his back to her for a second, not knowing what else to do. Then he felt that she would tease him for being bashful or a sissy, and he faced her again with sticky spit on his lips. His breathing sounded like the heavy rushing of a stormy wind. His heart jumped around inside him. He felt a craving to take off her cotton dress and to kiss her all over as she lay on the floor. "What you got there? A black an' blue mark? Where 'bouts did you get it?"

"A dern long time that you were a-noticing it." She pouted at him. "I did it when I was carrying the cream cans. You remember? When the wind blew my dress up, and you had such a duck fit about it?"

"Mmm."

"I would mmm if I was you. I could have torn my whole leg half off, and you'da never noticed it."

"Pretty bad bruised, ain't it? Yeah. Here. Lemme give it a nice good rubbin'. I'll kneel right down here between your feet just about right here, and, here, don't jump thataway now, an' I'll give you the smoothest an' th' nicest rubbin' job that any shemale ever got since Jesus quit paintin' little red wagons. But my old hands is so rough an' all cut up an' blistered an' warty an' so full of calluses that you might feel more like you was getting' runned over by a wild herd o' mean cattle." He kissed her kneecap.

"No such of a thing. Feels good. Owwch. Not so hard

right on that spot right there, there. Ohhch. Mmm. That's as nice as even a town girl could want. Leg might not be so pretty as a town girl's. Think?" She rubbed her hair against the wall as she talked, with her eyes half shut and her lips wet.

"Town gals ain't even in it." Tike's face looked hurt as he examined her blue muscle. "Ain't even in th' runoff."

"Ouch. Easier a teeny little bit. Now I do know you're a silly." She spread her feet farther apart. Tike kneeled between them and pushed her legs more apart with his knees. The warmth of his rubbing felt so good that she let her body fall as limber as a towel. "Now I'll tell you what a termite is," she said.

"Yeah?"

"A termite is something that eats up houses and makes things all rotten."

"Huh. All things rotten?"

"No. Just some things. Wood. Tar paper. Linoleum. Houses. Ahh. Gosh dern whiz a mighty gee ohh. Tike, you've not got the least idea how good the feel of your hands is to me now."

"Does he make dogs an' cats rotten?"

"No. Ohhh. I don't know." She half laughed to herself.

"Make people rotten?"

"Nooohhh."

"Just wood an' tar paper an' 'noleum? Huh?"

"Mostly just wood. Wood houses," she answered. "Most near anything that's built out of wood."

"Huh, mmm. Rub my hair back out of my eyes, will you, Hon? Can't see half of what I'm rubbin' here. Can't 'ford to miss out on none of it."

"None of what? Sil?"

"None of my leg I'm a-rubbin'."

"Your leg? Since when is my leg your leg?" Ella May tried her best to act serious. "Please state."

"Since the first time I ever rubbed it. 'Member?"

"No. And neither do you. Shut up. Keep rubbing." Ella May knew just how and when to toss her head and to cause her hair to fall down across her shoulders, so that with every rub, Tike's nose and mouth caught the smell of her hair and her neck, and caused his blood to warm up like a kettle on a cookstove. "Do you remember when it was?"

Tike swallowed a lump in his throat and said, "Strikes me it was one night, ah, that night, you recollect, when your ma and your pa had gone to bed and your three big brothers and your two little ones was all a-hanging around the front room there, keeping warm by the fire, and we held your mama's old dough board up on our laps and played poker for matches."

"Ooooooo." Ella bumped her head back so hard against the wall that the loose dirt sifted from cracks and little humps where the winds had packed the dust as hard and as tight as mud daubers or as hornets, ants, or wasps packing mud. The sifting of the dust down behind the wallpaper caused both Tike and Ella May to open their eyes a slit wider, to stare at nothing, but to listen and to think, and to let their history sift through their brains as the names of their peoples now sifted over the top sod. The only sound that was made was her high whine, "Oooooo." For that brief short second and space of time, the room was the room of a ghost house, and the spirit named in the winds tossed more and more dust, more and more dirt, into the air, to strike up and down against the house, like spirits of the dead carrying their own dirt, howling, begging, crying somewhere on the upper plains to be born again.

"I'd like to stay right here and rub your cuts an' burns an' bruises all night long, Lady, but I hear somethin' "—his face tilted up toward the ceiling—"I think I hear an awful funny sound out there in that wind." He kissed the bruise on her leg and said, "Plant, plant. Dig dig. Cover up, cover up. Now my seed's all planted an' dug down good an' deep for th' winter." He scratched her thigh muscle with one finger as if he were digging, then he made a movement with his hands as if he were covering it over.

As a rule every afternoon a few minutes before the sun went down, Tike struck out and fed his two hogs, milked his six cows, fed his four horses, and tossed a bucketful of mixed feed to his chickens while Ella May separated her cream, made biscuits and milk gravy, fried pork ham, and boiled a pot of coffee.

But she told Tike, "Methinks me hears me an awful strange note of kinda funny music in that wind meself.

Here. Jump up. Close that old no-account door before this house just fills up with air and blows off across the country like a balloon. Close it tight. Here. Throw on this heavy shirt and this jumper. Wait till I get on my Fifth Avenue rag coat here, and I'll help you do the outside chores, then, what say, huh, you help me get the cream separated and the supper fixed and then the dishes washed and all of the cracks chinked full of rags, huh? What say, huh?"

As they ducked their heads down and crossed the yard, Tike snarled and shook his head and said, "Whew. Grab a tit an' growl."

And Ella May scolded him, "I do wish that you would try to use better language."

All of the time that they worked at their jobs, Tike cursed, spit, cracked jokes, whooped and hollered, and made different sounds like the chickens, ducks, dogs, turkeys, geese, horses, cattle, and sheep. "Only lingo I ever could talk." He laughed at Ella.

He jumped his barbed-wire fence and threw a bucket of seeds out onto the ground, and while the chickens pecked it up in a thankful way, Tike flapped his arms and crowed like a rooster. The horses lifted their heads in the air and snorted, both at the wild yells and at the wilder winds in the distance. There was a wall-eyed worried look on the cattle's faces, and he bowed his neck, hunched his shoulders, and swung his head back and forth, as sad, as piti-ful, and as worried as any of the cows. He drove them into their stalls while Ella May poured buckets of feed into their boxes. She scolded at him again, "You could learn how to be something else besides a lunkhead. You could if you'd only put out the energy to try. But the trouble with you is, you won't even try."

"Try ta what?" he teased her as he milked his first cow.

"Oh." She milked her first one at the side of him, so that her back was only an inch or so from his. "Try to be a man, talk like a man."

"Gaddernit. Don't I talk like a man, Lady?" He lost his temper as he answered her. "Don't I? What in th' devil do I talk like then, if I don't talk like no man?"

And all of the time during the milking of the six cows, their argument went on. "Like a lunkhead. Like an old Star Route nitwit."

The sound of the wind against the hollow cowshed was loud in their ears. They raised their voices as they talked. The noise of things moving in the wind came to their ears like the flapping of wings. Dry stalks of corn, *higuera*, tumbleweeds, and sticker bushes rattled as they bounced against the boards, as they blew loose from their places and leaped, jumped, sailed, and whistled past the ends of the shed. The world moved around about them. All of the face of nature crept, crawled, wiggled, shook, watched its chance, and then howled away over the grass roots.

The top grasses, stiff stalks of weeds, bushes, brush of the plains, kept their place and held their footing, but seemed to sing and hum and cry, someway, somehow, as the other looser pieces of paper, hay, grass blades, silt, and straw left in the currents of the air. And to Tike and to Ella May, born and bred, lived and worked, fed and raised, loved and married, right here on these plains, to them, inside them, in their hearts this was a sorrowful season, an old and a dry season, a season of good-bye and parting, a season when all of the things of the plains, the twigs, grasses, hays, flowers, stalks, and the shucks, the things grown of the earth, take leave without further crying, and blow away somewhere to be whipped apart, to be parted and parted again. And the sadness in the high dark clouds and the sadness in the low biting winds was a big enough sorrow and a heavy enough sadness without adding any more onto it by whipping one another with wisecracking words.

In order to be funny above Ella May's scolding, Tike gritted his teeth as he drew the last drop from the tit of his last cow, and he spit down into the manure and straw underfoot and said, "You just wait till I get you back in that house, Miss Lady, I'll show you who's a man." He half closed his eyes and visioned what sorts of pranks he would play on her, he saw her cornered in the front room behind the lamp, and he imagined already that he heard her screaming and laughing, "Tike. Tike. Yes. I said yes. I said you was one. You're one. You're a man. You're a man. Ha ha ha ha ha ha ha. Donnnn't. You're a man. I take it back. I'll not say you're not one again. Tike. Tike."

These folks were the folks of nature. They were the son and the daughter of nature and their loud yells, screams, and laughs came from shouting back into the face of all men and all nature, and their quick minds were as quick as their fast tongues that always yelled down all men, all events, and all of the things of men and nature. They were back in the house again before either one of them spoke. The upper plains folks have fought for room enough out there to talk loud and to yell long-distance, and also to turn quiet and to have room enough to think deep. "Tike, you would just be under my feet and in my way trying to help me fix supper. I think you had better spend your time putting some more newspapers on the wall. I don't want you to cause me to spill this skillet full of hot grease all over myself."

"Do which an' how?" Tike set his two three-gallon buckets of new warm milk down on the floor. He opened his hand in the air to slap a cat away and said, "I'll knock your head off. You danged old lousy satchel, you!"

"Tike. Tike Hamlin." There was a fighting, peeved sneer on Ella's face. "What did you call me? I heard you. What did you say to me?" She lifted the hem of her apron to cry over the cookstove. The fumes of the asbestos wick starting to burn got into her eyes. She felt the pain shoot through her nose and head, but felt somehow glad that the fumes caused her face to be wet with tears. "You said you, said, said, that I was an old satchel, and, and, and that you, you would knock my head off! I heard you! I'll throw this kettle full of hot water all over you if you touch me!"

"Talkin' at th' cat." Tike grinned. "Gosh, dang a-mighty, dern, Lady, you didn't really think that I was gonna knock your head off, did you? Your head?" He hugged her close up against his dirty overalls and kissed her tears. "Did I fool you, Lady? Haw haw haw. I really had you kneelin', didn't I? Gosh? I got to have this little head to talk to and kiss on. Couldn't knock it off. But I shore did have you squawlin', huh? Hah."

"Was not crying."

"Not cryin'? Well, then, could you tell me what all of these here tears is doin' all over your face an' cheeks here?"

She fought away. "Fumes. They caused it. Not anything you said." She mopped her nose and cheeks and her eyes red and dry with her cooking apron. "Couldn't scare me. Not if you was as high as the moon and as wide as the sections, not if you had teeth like our old horse out there and a tractor motor and two wheat combines down in your guts. You're not so big as all of that. Mister Tike." She turned her back to work at her cooking. "Go do what I said. Did you hear me? I've got that dishpan in there full of flour paste and that little whisk broom for a brush. Hurry. Run. See how much you can put on before supper. Huh?"

"Ain't." Tike stood behind her and felt the heat get hotter from the burners. "Ain't not."

"And why? What? What are you saying? Go on. Don't stand here behind me and heckle me any such a way. Run."

Tike slid his hand under her arm and felt the nipple of her breast. "Lady."

"Tike. Your hand is cold. Don't."

"Lady."

"Quit. I'll chop your fingers off with this knife. Ohhmm.

Honey. Tike. I just can't stand your cold hands. That's all.
Go paste on some wallpaper so the house will be a little
speck warmer at least."

"Lady. I said, Lady."

"Lady what?"

"Turn around. This way. Gimme a big kiss an' hug."
He felt her muscles up and down her back and squeezed
her hips. "You know, Lady, somethin' tells me, Lady, that
you're goin' to hafta be a mighty tough lady to see this out."

"See what out?" She pushed her ear against his chest and
her stomach closer to him.

"See this. Just this. All of this."

"This? What all, say?"

"Oh . . . Lemme just hug and squeeze you closer to me
thisaway, Lady. I feel so good. So good when I feel you
close up against me. Keeps me warm." His head was bowed
and his eyelashes touched against the waves of her hair. "All
of this whole mess of stuff that I'm in. Stuff. Stuff like you
never was in before in your life. Kind of stuff you never did
see before. Mean stuff all around everywhere. Stuff I didn't
want to hit you with. I didn't want all of my old life to come
jumping down and run over you, Lady. I just wanted us to
be here, here together like this, longer than all of this stuff
takes to come and to go, and I been hoping that I'd be able
to keep most of it from hitting you and from hurting you,
and from making you any different than what you are right
now, and not old and mean and tough like a wild animal,
like you see some of the people around, and like I am some

of the time, or something like I feel in me all of the time, partly or mostly."

"I've not got the least worldly idea of what it is you are trying to say, Mister Man, but your words sound like your sense of all human reason has flew up on the windmill platform to go to sleep for the night. I'm tough, Mister Man. You'll one day find out just how tough I really am. Turn me loose and let me fix supper."

"We got something bigger than supper to fix." He blew his breath down into her hair. "Lady."

"I know we have, Tike." There were tears in her words as her mouth moved against his shirt. "Got a thousand worries and ten million debts and all kinds of sickness and wrong weather and all of this land to fix. Got to plow and plant more. Got to get a hold of machinery. Groceries. Things to wear. Oil to run us. And we now owe more than we can pay back in thirty years, even if the weather sobers up and the crops come good every season."

"And you never did have a worry, never did owe a copper red cent in your whole life before, not till you hooked up with this old mean no-good outfit of a Tike Hamlin," he said.

"Did I not tell you, please, please, please, Tike, not to ever let those words slip your tongue again? What are you about to beef about next, my old rich daddy? Stop. Don't kiss me anymore. I'm walking out. I'll yank this apron here off and I'll be out of that door and gone in two seconds. Just one more word. Just one little breath. Just one. My goodness gracious sakes alive. Goodness, lordness, Mathuzalem to jigsaw puzzles! God! Quit. Turn me loose. Go away. Get over there and paste those papers on the wall. Put them on about two or three thick, magazines two thick. You put my dress down! Mister, Mister Tike Hambone! Git!"

"Ain't gittin'."

"You are, too, or I'll whack you in two with this blade. I said get to papering!"

"No use to aim no little ole point of a knife at my guts, Lady. I ain't gittin', ain't budgin' out of my tracks till you tell me somethin'." He looked her in both eyes. "Tell me you'll pay me off in material."

"I'll not. Material?"

"Material."

"I'll pay you off with a glass of water and a toothpick."

"My kinda material."

"Me pay? You? How about you doing some of the paying? That paper on that wall will keep your old sore hide just as comfortably heated as it will mine. Why had I ought to be the one to pay you for the work? Say?" She acted hard, but she felt a soft, sandy feeling all through her, like the rainwaters eating away a patch of soil, like a farm washing grain by grain down with the rain, and up again with the dust. "Me pay?"

"No pay"—he shook his head and looked her whole body up and down—"no work."

"Why me pay?"

"You. I said you. I think you heard me say you." He held her closer and tighter against him. "See . . . ? Miss Lady?"

"But, but , but . . . I've not got any money."

"How sad."

"Not even fine clothes. Nor even any nice furniture. Nor a good car. Not anything that you would really want."

"So?"

"Only, only, say, some milk, and some butter, and some eggs, and a little handful of seeds of some kind. Not even a bushel of wheat, Mister. Not even, not even a drink of whiskey. Only some windmill julep, or something like that. I, ah, I, ah, just didn't happen to think to bring my check-book with me today." She twisted in a prissy movement and ducked her head as he hugged her.

"Milk an' honey's all right."

"But I, you see, ah, I sell all of my good milk. I separate it into cream and butterfat. After it goes through the separa-tor there, then all I've got left is old bluejohn skimmed milk. And you're such a high-society businessman that you'd not be at all pleased nor satisfied with my milk after all of the good things have been taken out of it. And, ah, as for honey, I've not got a single bee on this whole farm, that is, none of my own, they come here and suck all of the honey out of all of my nice pretty flowers, and then they fly away, *bbbzzzzzzzzttt*, like that, and take all of my nice good honey away to somebody else somewhere." She worked with her ham in the skillet, biscuits in the oven, coffee in the pot.

"Then you swear that so far as you know there ain't a drop of honey on this whole farm."

"Stack of Bibles. I swear."

"Well, ah, ah, then. Now, we'll just say, that, ah, as far as you're concerned, there ain't no honey about this place? Not even one little drop. That is, I mean, of your own?"

She answered with her back to him, "Not nary a drop."

"And as for the milk. Ah, now, you say that you send all of your good cream into town for butterfat and that what you've got left is just old weakly bluejohn thin stuff that you feed to the hogs an' to the chickens? That right?"

"Right as a fox."

"Well, now. Just what would you say if I was to prove to you that you are telling a great big, big lie, this big? This wide? An' this high an' this long? Wouldn't make you sore, would it?"

"Ohhh. No sir. You see. Sir. I've not been married to this landowner for so very long, sir, and sir, he sir, might sir, well he might not have told me, he might not have shown me, sir, where every little thing is. Possibly there's just oodles and gaboodles of milk and honey here, and butter, too, sir, for all that I would know."

"I see."

"I am glad, sir, that you see, sir."

"Still . . ." Tike tangled his fingers in the waves of her hair as it fell down from her shoulders. "Still, ahhh, you would like for me to do the common labor of papering your house with the latest newspapers, and you tell me there's not a drop of pay in it for me. Right?"

"Nary a drop."

"Now. Just wait. Right there. Wait. Ahhh. Now, what

if I go ahead and do this work? Ahh, would you say, then, that you would be willing to pay me a fair and a reasonable share of all of the milk and all of the honey that's not sent into town, I mean, all that is still left here?"

"All that is left?"

"Yes. After you send your regular amount on into town, just as you always have."

"Give you all that is left?"

"I said, a fair share, a fair share of what is left."

"What do you call a fair share?"

"A tenth part. Tenth of all's left." Tike still pretended a businesslike manner.

"Okay. All right. I'll do it. Go ahead. Get to work. But. Oh . . . Just one little thing." She held her chin up high. "You must agree that as a workman, as a laborer, as an employee, that you won't hinder me with my housework, nor get under my feet while I'm trying to do my farming here."

"You'll not even see me, Lady. Miss Lady. Good day." Tike pulled his hair up from the top of his head as though he were tipping his hat to be polite. Then he went through all of the moves and motions of getting astraddle a fine saddle horse, and said, "Whoa. Here, boy. Boy. Whoa. Whoa. Steady there, boy. Ahhh, Miss Lady, would you please tell me which a way it is over to that there job of work you was reeferrin' to? Hey, stand still, whoa."

She stood up on her tiptoes and pointed away across the room. "Oh yes. Just follow this fence line here. Just follow it on over yonder a ways, oh, not far, four thousand and

ninety-two miles, and then you turn off up that little year-
ling trail there, you'll see it bending out up over four mountains and a couple of pretty bad rivers if the ice is on. Just
about a half a day's jig trot for such a fine horse as you got
there."

"How'll I know th' spot when I come to it?" Tike
pranced up and down, up and down and around on his feet,
going through all of the paces, walks, gaits of his horse.
"How?"

"Well." She raised her voice as loud as to call across a
wide canyon. "You'll first see a big stack of old papers and
magazines."

"How old?"

"Shut up, you silly galoot."

"What next?"

"You'll run up onto a big old blue granite dishpan, with a
lot of the granite chipped off fifty or sixty years ago by some
of the right early settlers in this canyon here."

"Yeah?"

"Yes."

"Whoa boy. Stand steady, boy."

"You'll see a lot of flour and water mixed up in the old
dishpan."

"I eat that stuff?"

"No. You take that little whisk broom and you splash the
paste onto the wall, and then you take the papers and you
lay them up flat against the wall, and you sweep them down
hard and right real quick with the whisk broom. They stick

onto the wall. But just don't waste all of your time flirting with those pretty gals that you see in those papers."

"Cain't wait."

"If you get to feeling like you want to do any plain or fancy flirting, you'll do that with me. Nobody else. None of them old gals grinning at you like silly baboons out of those old magazines. You hear? See?"

"I see. Hear. Smell. Taste. Feel. Whoa boy. How about a little sample of what you got 'fore I strike out on this job?"

"Nope siree. Get going. Hit the trail. I'll yell for you after a while for your supper and then maybe a couple of minutes of flirting, but no longer than that, after supper."

"Whoa, boy, whoa," Tike shouted. "Can't hardly make this blame horse stand still when he hears about a job of work. Well, thanks, be seein' you." His voice shook the room, and his feet jigged up and down and rocked the old linoleum and the floor. He spent more energy dancing from the cookstove across the floor than he would have spent on the papering of five such rooms. He fanned his horse's ears with his imaginary hat, nodded to the left and to the right, smiled at friends and strangers along his way, jogged his feet twenty or thirty times just to move two or three feet. If the room had not been so small he would have danced all night. His blue shirt and faded overalls, as it was, were both somewhat soaked with sweat when he finally arrived at the place where Ella had left the stack of papers, the pan of paste, and the little whisk broom.

She laughed so hard that both of her lungs ached, and

in a few places she felt certain that the bones were cutting through her skin. She held herself with her elbows on the table, a knife, or a skillet, a great fork in her hands. She fell back against her wall at the side of the stove and laughed until she could not breathe anymore. She sucked her breath in through her mouth and tried to make signals or signs, tried to let Tike know, to ask him, to beg with him, plead with him with her hands in the air, with her fingers to stop his crazy comedy act. The more she lost her breath, and the more she ached and hurt in her belly, the more Tike wiggled his hips, his rump, the more he fanned his elbows up and down in the shadows that flickered from the cookstove where she laughed.

"Tiiiike, youuu craaazy," was just about all that she could command her stomach and her throat to say. Then she caved in again and bent over the back of a cane-bottom chair and hung her head down, closed her eyes, shook her hair, and burst out, "Ohh ho ho. Ohh ho ho ho. Ahh heee hee he he he he he. Stop!"

The room was a few feet larger than most of the rooms in the world, the reason being that the old-time settlers on these open upper flat plains did not feel like they were as crowded for space as are the dwellers on Los Angeles' Hill Street, Seattle's Pike Street, Duluth's Superior Street, Indianapolis's Senate Street, Chicago's Clark Street, Houston's Fannin Street, Buffalo's Beaver Street, Philadelphia's Spruce Street, nor as cramped and crowded as New York's Fourteenth Street.

The walls measured eighteen feet from one to the other, no matter which direction you ran your string. One window was on each side, and there was an east door toward the windmill and the barn, and a west door out across a hard strip of grazing land as flat and just about as wide open as the green cloth top of a billiard table. Yet eighteen feet is eighteen feet, or as long as six wide steps of a short-legged man when he's walking fairly on a beeline and comparatively sober. This was the vast and undying beauty, the dynamic and eternal attraction, the lure, the bait, the magnetic pull that, in addition to their blood kin and salty love for the wide open spaces and their lifetime bond to and worship of the land, caused not only Ella May and Tike Hamlin but hundreds of thousands and millions and millions of other folks just about like them to scatter their seeds, their words, and their loves so freely here.

And out of these hard-hitting millions of people, still, all in all, no other two of them were quite exactly like Tike and Ella May. None of the other millions of faces were like Tike's, and none of the other voices were like Ella's. And even though more millions of these little side-leaning, termite-eaten, rotting and falling poison houses are everywhere around you, still, none of these bent, warped, sagged, reeled, rocked, nor swayed in the same places as this one, nor did the holes, cracks, splits, slits, misfits, openings, crevices, come in exactly the same place.

Eighteen feet is eighteen feet by any ruler, any yardstick in the land, but some shacks will soak full of dampness and

rain and will spread out two or three inches in the course
of forty running years. Others will dry out, lose their gum
and rosin, and their natural sappy juice will get away into
the air, and the hot sun will beat down on all four sides of
them, and the dry winds will rip and tear at the boards and
scatter the shingles across the earth, so that, say, after the
same forty-odd years, this shack will shrivel up, and shrink
in size three or four inches.

Tike and Ella's shack did not come quite under either
one of these descriptions, that is, the wet one that swelled,
nor the dry one that shrank. It came more in the middle,
and suffered all the more because of it. It stood up against
the early spring rains that flooded the black gumbo furrows and made them look like the calm parts of the oceans.
These spring rains came just on the tail end of hailstorms
that pounded the green sprigs down with hailstones the
size of turnips, even the looks, the shape, of turnips. Car
tops are battered and the first leaves skinned off every stalk
and every growing thing. The waters of these storms flood
down out of the skies and chew the hard plugged mud into a
gummy slick black gumbo paste that stops all wagon wheels,
all auto wheels, all tractor wheels. These waters reflect the
colors of the clouds and the sun above for days and weeks
as they stand on the roads and on the fields, because there
are no man-made gutters here, no copper drains, no tin run-
ways, no iron manholes, to carry the floods off the flatlands.
Some, the soil drinks down to fill its veins, and some the
wind scoops up to get drunk on, a bit the horses, hogs, and

cattle drink down and splash in, and some the people stagger and bog along in. Still there are lakes and more lakes, flat, shallow holes of sky waters all over the plains, and the whiffs of the wind that blows off these waters feel like the forked tongue of winter.

These hailstorms, these floods, these falling and standing waters, all of them, every single drop of them, fell, sprayed, crashed, burst, exploded, and smashed into the grains of the planks and boards of Hamlin's little shack. And all of these soaked in.

Then the long keen rays of the late spring sun would come. They would shine down against the house for several hours out of every day. They sucked. They bit. They scratched. They clawed and they chewed at the boards. And they sipped the wild saps, gums, rosins, juices, and waters out again with sunrays, winds, the dry tongue and lips of the weather that sings, then whispers, then sucks, and kisses all of the little houses until they are dry again and brittle. And this was the dryness of the heat against the house.

No place on the earth is closer to the sun than these upper flat plains. No spot on the globe is closer to the wind than here on these north panhandle plains. Nowhere could the wind blow the rain any colder than here, nor any harder could the rain ever hope to fall, nor any longer could it stand. None of the world's winds blow dustier nor drier, nor harder day in and day out. Nowhere on the planet do the winds and the sun suck the grass, the leaves, the cattle, sheep, hogs, chickens, dogs, cats, people any drier. Nowhere could the winters blow any icier, the blizzards howl any lonesomer, nor the smoke from ranch house chimneys get whipped out any quicker, nowhere could the icicles hang down any longer, or could the whole world freeze in two minutes any glassier.

Just a flat place you call the upper north plains where ten blizzards and ten floods and then volcanoes had a big argument once and then hurricanes haven't been able to settle it yet.

Just a little thin boxboard shack in the land of grazing cattle, oil fields, carbon black plants, sheep herds, chicken farms, highways as straight as a string and as deadly flat as a frontline trench. A world of flat lands mainly. Flat, crusty, hard lands mainly. Some washed-out ditches deep enough to be young canyons and some gullies and some canyons big enough to swallow several of your big towns, cliffs and mesas, gorges and hollers, dry-bedded rivers, sand-bottom creeks, eggless hens, running ducks, stewball nags, hypocrite kilcustards, sons of virgin, hopping hare, buffalo bear, woolly sheep, tedious toddy drinkers, open mouthers, deep thinkers, beer makers, slop inhalers, dust and dirt eaters, and sandrock sleepers. Crawlers of the night soils, diggers under the sunny sod, hole feelers, hole diggers, hole makers, and hole ticklers. Easy gravel walkers and long tale talkers. The soul, the mind, the winds, the spirit of the upper flats, the flat upper panhandles, the winds of heavens unrolling, unfolding, and the listeners down below listening in two or three low brick buildings, wheeling chuck-a-luck, twenty-one, stud, blackjack, muley dice, racehorse mulers, fast nag tippers, coin flippers, vino fermenters, and curly hair sippers. Hair of the top plains. Soils of the dead grasses. Gravel hills, gravel hollers, doggy trots, buffalo wallows. Hens, hags, satchels, bags, the boasting, the knifing, the red-hot bragging. Brushy patch nippers, manurey skippers, backhouse generals, crooked cow trailers, sheep huggers, cheap sluggers, ewes and lamb dippers, sheep sleepers, and sheepy sleepers. You. Who. The winds and the clays dusted over graves of sixteen and sixty and nine in a row, nine in a line. On hoof or on the hook. On the trail or on the sledge. On the ice or on the fire. Hands between legs and stalks of bananas, truckloads of hot ones, and truckloads of produce, cabbage, beer, turnip, celery, eggs, squashes, reeling and rocking, trucks loaded with melons, feed her watermelon so she can't elope. Hair burned. Singed. Branded and scorched. Hide all blistered, and she's a burned-out sister. The upper flat plains.

Tike Hamlin knew the inner sounds and all of the outer sights of the things of the plains, his plains.

Belly band. Back band. Neck yoke and collar. Buckle it up. Snap it down. Carry it off and hang it up. Smokehouse. Woodshed. Cow stall. Manger. Henhouse. Big house. Backhouse. Cellar. Tap. Bolt. Nut and screw. Skinned knuckle. Cut finger. Burned arm. Scalded shinbone. Wheels. Hubs. Spokes. Seat. Brogans. Clodhoppers. Tit squeezers. Things of the barn and things of the pens and of the lots. Smells and the odors, sweet, sugary, syrupy, foul, rank, mean, and ornery. Hardheads. Stubborn heads. The loco cattle and bronco ponies. The penis of the stud slipping into the mare, and the sweaty hot open womb of the cow as she waited for the bull.

Ella May was of these things and born and raised among these things, and the life that she felt in her was the life that she saw and heard, felt, in all of these things in their seasons.

But the seasons of the summer things and the hot things were gone for this year, and this wind that was blowing its first hays and dusts across the farm was the very first touch of the winds of the cold season, the frosty-breathed, icy-tongued breaths of old winter. And here where no valleys hid them like cowards from the sun, or from the wind either, here where they hunted for no shelter behind rocks, here where they faced all of the ten million things that men and people and the weather could throw at them, here they both knew, Tike and her, that the difference between the summer and the blizzardy winter was sometimes, most times, just a couple of little short minutes. The tongue of the blizzard of winter licked under the flying tail of warm summer. One could go and the other could come in two minutes.

This was what was going on in the mind of Tike as he splashed his flour paste on the wall and pasted his papers down flat.

Ella May sat across the table from Tike and watched him eat his supper. She knew that a herd of deep thoughts were traveling through his mind. He looked down at his plate and he looked on through the plate. He looked at the dishes on the table and on through the dishes. He looked out across the room and his eyes went on through the walls. He looked out through the dark window and his eyes went all over the farm and through the panhandle. He looked across the plains. He spoke only a few words and the words seemed to go out across the country in the dark of the night. He smiled and looked into her eyes, and his eyes went in her and through her and on and on. Most of the time they talked about things at the eating table. There was a feeling of lonesomeness around the table when one of these quiet gazing spells came over Tike. Ella May felt Tike's feelings, though, and she knew that he had just let his troubles get heavier than his lips could carry. It caused her to feel sorry and she kept quiet.

She done the supper dishes while Tike spread more pages of magazines and papers over the walls. She set her pots and pans away in their orange-crate shelves on the south wall, then fixed the dishes on the table, covered them with a linen tablecloth, and said, "In a way, I'm always pretty glad to see the cold snap come, when it comes it kills out all my old bothersome flies."

" 'S right." Tike had gotten into the motion of flattening the pages against the walls, and he seemed to be angry deep inside him, so that he worked as fast as he could to try to fight back.

"Need a good hand there, brother Tike?"

"Yeah. Use one all right."

And together they whistled, hummed, sang parts and

pieces of songs, and Ella May held the papers flat while Tike pasted them down with his broom. Together they laughed at the old pictures of sharp-toed 1910 shoes. They hugged and laughed and pointed at square-built, clumsy models of automobiles with brass trimmings, squeeze honkers, and straps and buckles. They doubled over and held their bellies as they looked at the ladies in their hats, bustles, nets, and wigs. A well-dressed man in a white Palm Beach suit and a stiff straw hat caused them to go into laughing fits. They had looked through the papers and the magazines before, because Ella May had been saving them for several years. So their laughter was caused more by the wind outside, more by the shack and the sound of the dirt blowing against the sides, more by their actual hard luck, poverty, more by the debts and the worries, than by the pictures on the pages. They both felt that all of their fears and troubles were still not as silly nor as funny as these things in the papers of twenty years ago. Yes, both of them would have explained their laughing in these words, but the truth of the matter was that this was just one of those minutes, one of those hours, when the hurt of worry had hit its white-hot heat, and had simply melted and burned into laughs. If they had seen a kite in the sky, a cat on a fence, a boot in the alley, a dog with long hair, three trees on a hill, a weed out the window blowing in the night wind, they would have laughed.

III

AUCTION
BLOCK

One year. And what is a year? A year is something that can be added on, but it can never be taken away. Yes, added on, earmarked and tagged, counted in signs of dollars and cents, written down the income column and across the page with names, and photos can be taken of faces and clipped onto the papers, and the prints of the new baby's feet can be stamped on the papers of the birth, and the print of the thumb going back to work can be stamped onto the papers that say it is a good place to work. And a year is work. A year is that nervous craving to do your good job and to draw down your good pay, and to join your good union.

And a year of work is three hundred and sixty-four, or -five, or -six days of the run, the hurry, the walking, the bouncing, and the jumping up and down, the arguments, fights, the liquor brawls, hangovers, headaches, and all. Work takes in all climates, all things, all rooms, all furrows, all streets, all sidewalks, and all the shoes that tramp on them. The whirl and roll of planets do not make a year a year, nor the breath of the trifling wind, changing from cold to hot, forming steam back into ice. Oceans of waters that flow down from the tops of the Smokies and roll in the sea, they help some to make a year a year, but they don't make the year.

Tike had said to Ella May once before they were married, "What a year is, is just another round in our big old fight against the whole world." What he meant was his fight against the weather and against other men, and sometimes against his own self. But in his own words he was very close to right. He had a right, in a way, to say, "Our fight against the whole world," because it had always looked to him that his little bunch of people out there on the upper plains were fighting against just about everything in the world. He did not mean that, I, Tike Hamlin, am fighting against the world and all that is in it.

But Tike had it thought out to be a fight of an awful funny mixture. In a way, everybody and everything around him worked against him and fought against him. Yet in another way he did not exactly feel that this was so, because he knew that if and when things rose to a head or came to a showdown, his people on all four sides of him would do everything that they could do to help him. Some of them. Yes. Only some of them. To say that all of them would turn a hand to help him would be wrong, because he knew only too well that some of them would not stop to give him a sip of water if they found him lying with his mouth open at the side of some dry road. He had blood relatives that he had had many hot arguments with in the past, who had not spoken to him nor him to them in twenty years. And each time the calendar rolled another year around, both sides only turned more proud, and more cold, and more silent.

Ella May's most awful pain in this world was to have to ask for help from her people or from Tike's. Her old daddy had smiled and told her that when Tike and his wild ways brought her to the door of starvation, he would help her out with land, with tools, with a loan of money. He had said, "Every year that comes and goes you'll fall down a little lower an' a little lower. Ohhh. I know you young squirts are full of fire an' tarnation, an' you think that you can do all of yer own thinkin' on yer own hook. But I'll just set here on my front porch or somewheres around th' house an' wait till you come a-crawlin' an' a-whinin' back for me to help you. You'll belly down in th' middle of th' floor here like a little whipped puppy dog." And she had never seen his face since she spit at him and answered, "You and your old farm and your old stony house here will dry up and rot and turn into burnt powder and blow away into thin air before I'll set my foot inside your gate again! I wouldn't let your money bury me if I was dead!"

Tike and Ella May would have given their last spoonful of flour or of sugar or their last stitch of clothes to certain of their people who had always seemed to work, to save, to fight, to really try. Certain others, they knew, would only "blow the money on some fancy duds" or "scatter it by the handfuls in all of the whorehouses" or "get rid of it hangin' around that corner drugstore tryin' to work up a hunk of nooky," or worse yet, "go shovel it away on them old cards or dice or dominoes!"

And still it was harder than this to see through. The ways and the laws that people used to judge one another did not lie in any one certain mold. The people knew the other people. They knew the all good, the half good, the three-fourths good, and the nine-tenths good. One would have six faults and no good. Another had three good habits and four bad ones. Another had eleven sins and twelve virtues. This one, two vices and one streak of honesty. The next one, fair in some things and no-account in others. The next one, all right when the wind is in the east. The next one was a good man while his wife done his thinking. Another one was a hard worker but trailed loose women. And others had their own mixtures of the good and the bad and their makeup was as well known to the others as the times to plow and to plant and to cut and to gather. There were a few people around who fought, drank, gambled, fornicated, trifled, told lies, and cheated, but were so outright and so honest about it that Tike and Ella May either one would lend them their last coin or feed them or shelter them at any time, because they paid them back sooner than lots of the ones that claimed to be so holy.

And so the year went around. The wheel of time rolled down the road of troubles. They had the same things hit them day after day. The same cows bawled to be milked every sunset, and bawled to be milked again at every sunrise.

The same cackles of the chickens and the same crow-

ing of the roosters, and even if the chickens died or were
told to be killed, Tike's ear could not tell very much of a
difference in their cackling and their crowing. Each grunt
of his old mama and papa hogs he knew like a blood rela-
tive. Every little sniff and every little squeal of the baby
pigs Ella May knew like children in her nursery. The chirps
and the squawks, the sounds of little baby turkeys growing up, she knew, because she had carried each on into the
house and talked as she kept him down in a box of rags to
look him over, to see if he was all right, just to have some
company. It was the same with the new dogs, puppies,
the older ones running away, the shes that got in heat and
lifted their tails, ran, with all of the adult hes chasing after.
The same, too, with the young colts, calves, rabbits, dens
of baby snakes, ants, nests of naked little newborn mice,
and drunk-looking baby birds born somewhere on the flat
ground under a weed, and the same way with the families
of scratching cats, and kittens that make noises like a water-
logged organ. Jobs to do at the same time every day. Rocks
carried and thrown into mudholes. Wire fences patched up
and put back together again. Windbreaks for the animals.
Fences to stop stickery weeds and fences to cause the snow
to drift away from the livestock. The going. The coming.
The naked hours somewhere in the sun. Naked nights hit
in the bed from the wind. Laughs. Tears. Fun. Worry. Misery. Company. Lonesomeness. The wheeling of the moon
and the stars, whirling of planets, howls of the brave coyotes
and wolves, and the tracks of cougar, lion, and panther in

the cow pen. Blistered hands. Calluses. Back bending. Back breaking. Aching muscles. Sweat. Toothache. Headache. Stings. Things that hurt and things that feel good. This is how the year went. This is where it went. These things, and not a clock on a wall, make a year.

Ella May washed her supper dishes and threw the pan of dishwater out the west door in the dark. She felt the sting of the bite of the cold wind on her wet hands. "You know, Mister Tike, I'm always glad to see the first cold snap of weather come. It kills out all of my old mean biting flies. Most of them are already gone, I mean the ones outside, but there are still a few smart-aleck ones that live in here by the fire and hang on till the very first freeze." She rubbed her hands together in a towel to warm them up, and asked him, "Need a good work hand, to help you paste that paper over those old cracks?" She smiled and stood by the table. "Say?"

Tike grunted an answer. His mind had been wandering around the world nine times. "Hmm? Oh. Ahhh. Work hand? Naww. Lady, you set down there on the bed or somewhere and get you some rest. Set down before you fall down." Then he stood back and looked at the newly pasted pages that he had put on to cover the cracks. "Gad dern my soul to hell, anyhow, and tie up th' tails of forty tomcats! I've put enough flour and water on these walls to feed and raise and fatten six kids to butcher!"

"Only way on earth to ever keep out that old dust and wind, though, at least that I know of." She started to walk toward him to help him.

"I told you to set down before you fall down!"

"But I can help."

"You're so big an' round and so fat with that baby in your belly that if you fall down, Lady, you'll get started rolling and I never would be able to catch you. Set down. Make yourself miserable." He pointed his paste broom at a chair. "You know as well as I know why I'm tellin' you. Set down."

"But. Tike."

"Don't But Tike me! You know why. That baby was supposed to of been here four or five days back! It's liable to come jumpin' out across here with a tractor in each hand any minute now! He's comin' so late that he'll be grown up before he's even born! Set down. I don't want your blood on my hands. Not now. Not just when I'm on th' start of gettin' to be a big landowner. Set down. If he falls out there in the middle of th' floor he'll break his head!" Tike wore a faded old blue shirt stuck down into a pair of khaki work pants, and his same pair of heavy work shoes that he had on a year ago, only he had nailed new rubber tread soles onto them and kept them good and full of grease. "Just about through with this contract anyhow. Don't need no work hands. Guess I'll hafta print me a big sign an' put it up: No Work Hands Wanted So Keep To Hell On Traveling!" As he waved his whisk broom in the air he threw drops of the paste, which lit on Ella May's face, on her eyelid, and some in her hair.

"Tiiike. You old clumsy thing you. Donnn't. Will you

or will you not ever learn how to be careful?" The springs of the bed screeched with rust when she sat down to rub her face with her hands. "Old mean thing."

"Turn th' radio on. Play me some music." He nodded at her. "I got a damned tender soul. I need perty music jumpin' down all aroun' me here while I'm a doin' my work."

Ella May lifted the weight of the baby in her stomach and went over across the room to connect the naked ends of two wires that would make the radio play. She grunted in a good-humored way as she walked, "Oho hum hummy hummy hummm."

"No! You set back down over yonder on th' bed! I'll tie them two wires together!" Tike splashed more paste about the room as he waved his broom. "Oughta be able to take a reg'lar bath in some awful good music ever' day an' ever night for a hunderd an' seventy days."

As she sat back down on the edge of the bed, she worked at the knobs of the radio. It was an old one, in a green metal box, and the loudspeaker stood up on top of the box like an air ventilator on a ship. As Tike hooked the two wires together, Ella May looked at the speaker and worked the handles. Tike had put the radio close to the head of the bed so "Lady could just lay there with 'er baby in 'er arms an' lissen."

"I don't see what ever did possess you to go and give that much for such an old junk heap as this, anyway," she scolded at him in her soft way as he spit on his fingers and smoothed down a little hump in his wallpaper. "Why did you ever?"

"Goshamighty whizzers, Lady, that ain't too much to pay for a good radio. An' that's a good one. I seen an ad in a big magazine that said so. Company speaks mighty well of it."

"Yes. I should suppose the company would. I would too if it made me a millionaire and rich." She held her right hand up over her left breast and bent over with a stitch of sharp pain. When she saw that Tike's eyes followed her, she lifted herself up straight again. This little sharp cutting pain had been over her left breast now, coming and going, for months. In her own mind she traced it back to that day when she had carried the cream cans across the yard, and Tike had punched her with the sharp bone of his elbow. It had been there ever since, but not so bad that she had ever told him about it. Once or twice he had seen her bent over with the hurt and he had asked her what it was. She passed it off as just some kind of a regular female pain that all women have when their breasts swell at their monthly period. His eyes were faster and sharper in these days since the baby was in her, and he had got to where he did not trust what she said anymore about pains because she always moved her shoulders and passed it off as nothing. He kept his eyes on her until she felt nervous.

" 'Smatter over there?" he asked.

"Oh, just little stitches in my muscles here and there.

When I get bent over, I can't hardly get straightened back up again. Go on with your project. Don't worry so much about me."

"Just what in the hell else would you say I oughta worry about then, Missy?" He sounded like he held her in suspicion.

"Your work. Ahhh. Ding bust this dad-ratted old dod-rotted radio to the south pole and back, anyhow! Tike! Did you fix those wires together good?"

"Good as they'd go. Why?"

"Ohhh. I don't know." With her fingers she combed her hair back out of her eyes. "All I can get out of the old thing is just this crazy rattling sound and this infernal screeching. And I do honestly believe to my soul that this is going to force my brain to just stop and quit functioning completely!" In spite of the fact that she did try to sound humorous and fresh, there was a tired drag in every word that she spoke. "Could it be that the wires up on top of the house are knocked down or something? Something. I don't know. It's just not working. Maybe it just doesn't like me."

"Ya gotta talk good to it."

"I guess it's just got it in for me."

"Treat it nice. Talk to it like dice. You gotta talk all kinds a super spucious words to it."

"Super spucious? What kind of words are those?" There was a hollow look about her jaws as she studied the radio with all of her mind. "Super what did you call them?"

"Spucious. Spucious. Don't you know? You mean to set

there an' tell me that you're a great big grown-up womern, old enough to have a baby in your gut, an' you still don't savvy what super spucious is?" He put on an expression of great self-importance and held his elbows out to his sides like a family butler.

"Well, then, sir, if you happen to be so familiar with matters of this nature, then in all probability your efforts and not mine will meet with the most success in our maneuvers to coax this machine to play," she said, bowing to him. And there was a flirty look in her eyes as she said again, "Maybe you could tell me just what about your super spucious words are. And just where about did you learn them?"

"Grampaw Hamlin taught 'em to me, one at a time on th' shortest day of ever' year way down in a slick-off canyon of th' Cap Rock cliff." He marched over with his brush in his hand and a proud look.

"And sir. Just what are those words?"

"Words you use to make all kinds a forces an' powers come down to one little spot an' go to work for you an' do whatever you tell 'em to. Brings all of th' invisible forces down to work on th' visible ones."

"My. My. My."

"It's th' words of th' dead civilizations an' th' civilizations that ain't even been born yet. You gotta know just how to go about it. Brings th' past an' the' future down to work on th' present."

"The past and the future down to work on the present?"

"I don't say nothin' super spucious but once."

"Well. Do say."

"Yeahh. Perty handy thing to know. You know."

"Well, I should daily remark."

"Ahhhh. Here. Let me have that knob. I'll get some noise out of that contraption. Here. You hold my wallpaper brush. I don't want to gum the thing all up with paste. Ah-hhemmm. Now, let me see. Let me see. Now, let me see."

"Go ahead and see. I'm not hindering you, am I?"

"Where's that set of directions that come with this outfit?"

"They are right there in that little book hanging on that nail." She pointed.

Tike reached out his hand to get the book of instructions. "Ha."

"I thought you said that you said you were going to use your super spucious magic to make it play. You don't need that little old book of directions. Call your powers down to go to work on it." She looked at him with a tired, sad smile.

"Hogey hogey hogey hogey hogey, dogey dogey dogey dogey, hogey hogey hogey riz a riz a radio, play! Play! Play!" He held both hands over his head and danced around, kicking one foot against the linoleum. As his toe struck down against the dry, rotted, flaky thin worn linoleum, a cold shiver went through his whole body, and his face and his skin became wet with a chilly sweat. As he whirled and said his magic words, the floor, the walls, the whole house moved and trembled, and the loose dust made a loud noise as it sifted down behind the dry wallpapers. He kept dancing. He smiled. His eyes turned into lights and were half shut as he danced. For a few moments his wrists ached and his fingers burned and he felt a craving to take his two fists and beat the whole house down, take his two feet and kick the odd pieces out into the night. He knew that he could do it. Not a plank nor a board on the whole house could have stood up under one good crash of his shoulder, and most of them he could have rammed through with his bare fist. He was thinking to himself, "I'll do it. I'll do it. I'll scatter its carcass all over these upper plains! This measly shack cain't keep my woman an' my baby on a ball an' chain."

Ella leaned her head back against the fancywork of the iron bed rail. She heard the house shake, the wallpaper crack some more, the dust sift down and down and on and down and down. She smiled. She felt Tike's craving to crash it in. She sat there, leaned her head back, and smiled, but there was a vacant spot, an empty place somewhere there across her face. Tike saw that, and this was what made him have his raging desire to just shut his eyes and double up his fists and just whale away and batter the whole thing down into a trash pile and then strike a match to that. He still danced. He whirled. He jigged. He waved his arms above his head, and fanned them at his sides, he whooped, yelled, and made gobbling noises with his hand over his mouth. It was not that he wanted to dance, it was not that he enjoyed it nor got any fun out of it, but it was because it was keeping that last little trace of Ella's smile on her face there. And it seemed that he had got started and just could not stop. He hollered himself hoarse, and worked his clothes into a suds of sweat. He cursed the angels, the devils, the spooks, the saints, the tides, the seasons, and everything else above and below the earth, but all of these he cursed to himself under his breath. He cried out his super spucious words, "Oolagy, dooley, moola katolly, hobity hotine, hobity hotine!" Then he waved his fingers into the speaker of the radio and said, "Plazay! Plazay! Plazay!"

Ella looked into the speaker.

"Play!"

She kept looking.

"Play!"

"Pulllay!" she helped him out.

Tike fell down tired on the floor and hugged her legs as she sat down on the bed. He put his head sideways into her lap and breathed like a tired dog after a swift chase, his clothing soaked with large spots of perspiration as he rubbed his hard hand over his wet cheek. He was so out of wind that he could hardly talk, but finally did manage to say, "Playyy!"

Ella May's voice sounded thin and a long ways off. "Play."

A hum, a scratchy rasping blur of noise, a rattle, a whine, a clicking, clacking, several high and low zooms, far-off rumbles, sobs, sighs, and then a terrible clatter came from the mouth of the loudspeaker. This was the only answer that it made to all of Tike's sweating and working and dancing.

"Guess," he said between gasps of air, "guess, guess, maybe th' battery's run down."

She felt his hair and cheek and chin with the ends of her fingers and asked, "Didn't old Grandpa Hamlin teach you any super spucious words about how to charge batteries again?"

"Yeah. He did." He shook his head in her lap and pulled his shoes up under him. "He showed me some. Works ever' time."

"Then why don't you get up there and say them and dance them and yell them and scream them and charge these old batteries again?" she asked.

"Well. Ah. Just to tell you a fact for a fact"—he panted as he thought—"ah, th' super spucious words an' the dancin' that it'd take to recharge them old dead batteries is, ah, well, perty hard. Fact is, ahhh, I believe, believe it'd be a little easier just to carry them batteries into town an' th' man run 'em up again on his reg'lar machine."

It was after several minutes of stillness in the room that Ella said, "You know it was certainly nice of Blanche to stay here with me these last few days."

Tike had rolled a cigarette, spilled loose tobacco in the wrinkles of his pants, and turned to face the room and to lean his head back against her knee. She smelled his khaki pants and blue shirt filled with his sour sweat, mixed in with the smoke that he blew from his mouth as the cigarette hung down from his lips. She heard him blow smoke without moving the cigarette, and heard him say, "Yeah . . . Really sure 'nuff was. You're a dern daggone fool, though, Elly, to let her leave you alla these four or five hours. Kid was to poke its head out right now, shucks, I wouldn't know which a way to jump. Where did you say that she went?"

"Into Jericho to buy some things. She'll be right back. It's not more than nine miles by the new shortcut road. I look for her right now any minute. Of course it is getting dark, all right. And I would feel just a touch better if she would come. But, you know, Tike, she has just been the nicest thing that you ever did see."

He shook his head and listened. "Yeahhh."

"And besides, Mister, you could use a few more brains than you've got right now, yourself. You could even learn how to welcome a little newly come baby into the world your own self. Old Grandma and Grandpa told me they brought two of theirs in without the help of any doctor."

"You're nuts."

"Why? Wouldn't you like to be the first human to shake hands with this little fellow? Tell him howdy, give him a good friendly sendoff in the world?" She laughed. "I would really like to see you, Old Tike Hamlin, reaching and snatching and fretting and fuming and foaming and jumping around all over the place! Ha ha ha ha!"

"You're a downright liar an' th' truth ain't in you," he shot back at her. "You're lyin' an' you know you're a-lyin'!"

"No sir. But that Blanche is really just about the sweetest and the nicest one woman that anybody anywhere would ever hope to see. Why, do you realize that she just won't hardly let me turn a hand to lift a thing, to pull at anything, to heave nor to tug, nor to bend nor to stoop, nor to bounce around nor shake up and down nor to strain myself in any way, shape, form, or fashion? She is certainly fine. And she hasn't left my sight now for ten days until just today. I think that she gets letters from a sweetie and she doesn't want us nor any of her folks to know anything about it. And so she didn't have him to send them here to the farm, but rented her a box of her own in Jericho. She thinks that the box will be just running over with all kinds of sweet things from him, and, well, I certainly don't blame her for wanting to go. Of course, this is all just what I think. I might be wrong. But I have watched her slip letters out from under her apron and read them and then hide them real quick again before I noticed her, or before she saw me. So she walked up to the road and caught the mail carrier going in, and she got in and rode with him. She said that she could catch some of the ranchers coming back out. She seems to know just about when everybody in this whole country does their buying in town. This is Thursday and I do know that the Pitzer folks and the Steins go in with their cream and eggs. She'll get out over there on the Sixty-Six just a mile, and it won't take that Blanche girl but just about three hips and a couple of hops to come a-bouncing in at that old door right there. She might be feeling so good from her letters that she will just about run the whole house down when she does burst in. I look for her any minute now."

Tike listened and thought to himself, "I sorta do hope

that she rams this whole joint right down flat, smack, smooth against th' ground."

"What did you remark? Sir?"

"I said, I sorta do hope that she bangs this old house down when she comes in at th' door, like you was a-sayin'." The smoke from his cigarette mixed in with his words. As she saw the back of his head, neck, and ears in his cigarette smoke and in the lamplight, the moving smoke caused him to look like he was flying across the earth. The smoke that he blew down between his legs along the floor rose up and formed into little flat clouds four or five feet above the linoleum. The clouds moved, lay to one side, slipped, fell away and rose up again, and waved like the waters of the oceans.

She felt her old feeling blow down, rise again, form into the shapes of clouds that blew and waved, then got whipped to pieces, knocked apart, smeared out by the drafts of the wind that sifted in through the cracks. Her thoughts were all wrapped up inside her in one tight bundle as she sat watching the back of his head. She saw other visions of him in the whipped-out smoke in the room. Him lifting, bending, and him stooping, crawling. Him running and sitting down alone and quiet. She saw again all of the old pictures. She saw a picture of him on the first day that she had seen him. Yes. He rode a fast bareback broomtail pony up along a hard dirt road, and he waved his hat and yelled so loud that he caused her buggy team to snort and run wild. She saw him working thrashes, binders, carrying water to work in a rag-wrapped jug. She saw him taking tractor and car motors apart, and then putting them back together again. She saw him laughing and playing with her daddy's dog in the yard while he put one over on the old man and let her ease out the back door. She saw him all up and down the cliffs and gullies of the Cap Rock. She sat there with a blank stare and saw Tike Hamlin doing just about everything that a man ever done.

She leaned her head over in a new position against the bedstead and folded her hands over his forehead, and she sighed, grunted in a tired way, and said, "Tike."

"Mmm?" He smoked.

"Everywhere that you look, do you see me?"

"Huh? Oh. Guess so. How come you to ask? Yeah. I guess I do. I guess I do at that. Hmm. Never did just think of it like that before, but I reckon since you mentioned it, I s'pose that I do. Why?"

"Oh, I don't know. I was just leaning back here, enjoying of my aches and miseries, and just thinking."

"Ha."

"Just thinking that I've always seen you in this way."

"Ha."

"I always did. And I don't really know why. When I look out across the country I see you. Out across the farm I see you. Out across the room here I see you. And I guess that the experts that know about such things would say, Oh well, it is just because I loved you. And so I guess it is. I guess it is why. But I'm just sitting here and thinking."

"Yaaa."

"Wondering."

"Mmm-hmm."

"Just trying to figure. Just figuring and figuring and figuring. Trying to figure out just some one little teensy-weensy reason why I should have to love you so much."

"Ha. Ya. You got me fooled there, Lady." He squeezed his hands together so nervous and so hard that she could hear his bones and gristles crack. "I never could figure out that one myself. Listen. Listen." He leaned his head toward the radio. For some unknown reason the speaker had gotten quiet, and it was for some few minutes that they listened to the sounds of an orchestra. It was so soft that they strained their ears to hear, because of the dead batteries, but the notes of the music were easy to hear. It was the horns and the saxes, hot trombones of a Saint Louis dance band playing some dreamy, bluesy Louisiana ragtime. The shuffle of the trombone and the blare of the little wet trumpet sounded jazzy, wiggly, fiery, and Tike saw people all around the world move their hips and rub their bellies.

"Hotch chh chh chh. Hot choochy, choochy. Shew. Shew. Shoo. Shooo. Wowww. Whow. Whow. Whow. Whow." Ella May only rocked her head from one side to the other, and tapped the end of her shoe in the air under Tike's back. He leaned against her so as to feel every movement that her body made in time to the music.

And then it stopped. And he said, "Boy, howdy, Lady, you was right in th' right church an' th' right pew an' th' right row with th' right how, an' a-goin' an' a-blowin' right on down to Georgia that time, wasn't you?" He moved his shoulders against her legs and knees as he sat on the floor.

"Shh. There's a man speaking. Let's see if you can hear just what it is he's crowing so about." She tapped him on the head.

And they held themselves stiff and still for the next few minutes, because the static noises again had just about whipped the voice of the man to pieces. The wild elements, rays, and magnetisms, the unharnessed and unseen, invisible forces of the plains bit and clawed and chewed at his words exactly as did the ears of the two that sat there and listened. And there were parts of his words that the weather whipped to pieces, and there were other parts that Tike and Ella May beat into dry sand.

"Shh."

"Yeah. Shh. Shush."

"Don't you shush me. Hush."

Tike stood for a few seconds, brushed the loose crumbs of tobacco from his clothes, and blew his breath down against his shirt with a whistling noise. He felt Ella's hand take hold of his little finger on his left hand and the warmth caused him to feel again all of the bitterness and the coldness of the night outside. The moisture of her hand was warm. He kept his ears to the speaker. Then, without making any noise, he sat down on the bed, leaned against the wall, and pulled her hand until she laid down at his side. She kept her ears to the things that the loudspeaker said. Tike held her around her waist with one hand and with his other hand he felt, rubbed, caressed, the baby in her belly. It jumped, it moved, it fluttered, it stuck its elbows, arms, and knees against her like a wildcat trying to fight its way out from under a box. The movements of the baby caused Tike to feel such a fear as he had never felt in all of the days of his life. Such a fear as he had never known that he could feel. A terrible lost feeling, a dread, a misery, a complete feel of being helpless, ignorant, and fooled. Already this thing in her fought to get her attention for twenty-four hours out of every day, and already it beat her, fought her, struck her with its fists, and kicked her with its feet to get more and more of her love and her attention. Already. And it was not even a living human being yet. No name yet. No papers yet with its picture and fingerprints clipped on. It had not hoed a row, nor had it plowed a single furrow. It had not scratched the top sod, it had not touched a finger to the earth to cover over a seed. Had not driven a tractor down a row. Had not carried in one single solitary bucket of milk or water, nor done any work on the house. It had not done anything. Nothing. Not a single useful lick of work. And yet already, ahead of time, this far ahead of its own time, already it beat around, struck out with its fists, kicked, punched, and thrashed around just for the one sole purpose of getting everybody's attention, just for the one reason of causing everyone to run, to worry, to stumble and to fall, to move along faster, to go here, to go there, and skid around, just to hurt, to whip, to make trouble, and more gray hairs. This all taking place on the inside of her belly. For goodness sake, what on earth would the new stranger want and how much more would it yell and scratch and fight for its own self when it would get its head on the outside?

Tike was afraid to think any more about it. He shook his head to cause his thoughts to shift over onto other things. God. Lord. Jesus. Little prairie dogs and tarantulas. Lord God and all of you tangle-headed saints. Christ O Jeez O Lordy O Mighty O! He shook his head several times. The springs of the bed made so much noise that Ella May finally said, "Hush. Man talking. Listen. He's some kind of a big Government man. Put my dress down."

"Wanta feel. Brat a jumpin'," Tike said in a whisper so as not to interfere with what the big Government man was driving at. "Jump. You little monkey, you. Ha ha ha ha."

"Tike. Please. Be still. I'm listening. This man is a man from the Government."

"Yeah?"

"Yes. Listen."

There was an educated sound, a sound of the rattle of papers and pencils, in the man's voice. It was a bit of a boomy voice, a voice that had rehearsed, practiced for hours and hours every day to sound boomy and big, so it would find a little place somewhere in their ears to plant its seeds and to sprout its roots. A good-old-boy sound. A real old-crony sound. A right-hand-man, a brotherly and sisterly sound. A smooth, soft, oily running sound in the flow and the dance and the weave of the words. Tike smiled a bit of a mocking grin and whispered, "Don't he sound perty?" Ella May jabbed him with the point of her elbow and got quiet again.

And the voice said:

"And this, this appears very plainly to me to be the only answer to our problems!"

Tike pooched up his lips and shook his head wisely, as if to say, "Well, is that right?"

"In view of the world market, we have far too many hogs! Far too many sheep! Far too many cattle! Too much cotton. Too much corn. And too much grain of every kind. Our storage bins are running over, and we've got too much wheat!"

Ella May's stomach moved with the baby as she stuck out her lower lip and mocked, "Far, far, too much."

"It is a very plain and simple problem with a very plain and simple answer. Our modern machines and our modern factories and our modern systems of labor have simply given us more of everything than we can use. There is no demand for this oversupply. Prices are falling because all of the storage rooms are full and overflowing and nobody will buy the excess. There is too much. Too much of everything."

And a look that was half hate and half silly, a grin that was more of a sneer on Tike's face. Outside he heard the rattle of the cold wind against the dry house. He thought of the years that he had raised growing things, and said, "Oh yeah? Too much."

"It is better for you to receive two dollars a bushel for a thousand bushels of wheat than to raise three thousand bushels and have to sell it for thirty cents. And don't feel too hopeful when I tell you thirty cents, because I can quote you county after county right here in the wheat belt where it is going at just twenty cents a bushel and not one penny more."

"Ha," Tike said.

"Hmm," Ella May said.

"So in closing, I want to urge you to go along with this plan. The agent will soon come around and knock on your door with all the necessary papers. You simply agree not to plant a certain number of acres, and you are paid so much an acre for the acres that you leave idle. The price is different according to the kind of crop that you last planted on this land. The same goes for the meat animals that you kill this year and the ones that you agree not to raise next year. Your agent has all of the papers, with all of the classifications and all of the rates, figures, and prices. Remember, you are not being forced to leave your land idle nor to kill off your cattle nor your sheep nor your hogs. You are not being forced. You are not being driven. Most farmers have already signed up. Many of them have already received their checks. They say that they used their money to pay off some of their back debts so as to be able to borrow more money to run their farms in the years to come. Many intend to buy fertilizer and put their idle soil into better condition. Many will repair their houses, sheds, buildings, and barns. Many will build new ones."

Static sighed and moaned and the voice on the radio was blown away like a sky full of loose hay.

"He says that we have got too many of the blessings of life." Ella May held Tike's hand against her stomach.

"Yeah," Tike answered in a sour drawl. "Too much."

"I may have just failed to find them. Or possibly both of us overlooked them. When that agent comes around with those papers, I aim to ask him to come all around over this farm with me, and see if he can find all of these blessings and all of this oversupply of meat and things to eat, and things."

"What about all of these electric washing machines and ice boxes that you've got here in your little cottage, Lady? And what if he would find all of those trunks and suitcases and handbags full of all your nice perty clothes?" Tike's eyebrows went up and down like a private detective. "What then?"

She smiled in the light of the lamp and bumped her head against the wall. "That is right. Yes sir. No sir, you know, that is one thing that just did not enter my mind. He would be sure and certain to find my two limousines under the house."

"Sure he would."

"And those last two airplanes that I bought and hid up on top of the barn."

"Find them, too."

After being quiet for a time, her ear caught the sound of the radio at her back. It was still buzzing. It hummed like a long, flat stick thrown at a horse. There were horses in their minds. There were whole herds of horses born and raised on the plains, the sheep pony with his fast quick trot, the cow pony able to stop on a nickel and whirl on the point of a needle. There were herds and herds of bawling cattle kicking up their manure dust. There were the farms filled with hogs, sheep, cattle, horses, in their brains. These things moved in Tike's brain as if he flipped through a movie magazine with his thumb and saw the shapes and faces jump, cavort, flicker, and fade. Ella May saw long new furrows of good plowed ground and her nose smelled the roots, the syrups, the saps, the juices, not only of the ground but, too, of popping seeds with big white roots, drying stems and stalks and leaves with roots as hard as her fingernails. Already, without the slightest doubt, these wondering worried pictures, too, were moving across the closed eyes of the little new upper plainsman that fought under the weight of Tike's hand. And this was her feeling. A funny one, not any too clear a feeling, it was blurred and smeared as she tried to see it in her mind.

"You know"—Ella May started to talk—"I'm not really afraid that this business of killing of these animals and letting all of this land go idle will actually be the death of me, because I really feel like I will live through it. But I'm just laying here trying to figure."

"Figure what?"

"Trying to figure up what I'm going to say to this little varmint inside me here when he or she or whoever it is asks

me why it was that we ever did let ourselves do such a silly
old trick."

Blanche did come in at the door like everybody hoped, and
she did bring a swarm of the cold wind with her. The quick
change in the temperature in the room caused the pasted
wallpapers to crack all around the walls. Whirls of dust and
dirt circled across the floor like whirlwinds dancing above
the ground. Blanche was a large girl, full built, full breasted,
and several years younger than Tike or Ella May, and even
though she was of larger bone and limb than they, she was
faster, more limber, more active than they were. It was due
to her restlessness that she was so active, for she loved to
keep on the move and hard at work, day and night. When
Ella May and Tike slowed down or sat down, Blanche kept
moving all about the place doing everything that her eyes
could see to do. And her eyes usually found plenty that
needed doing around and about this place. The past few cold
and freezing days had partly driven her in from chores she
had found, invented, and made up to keep her busy on the
outside, so she put all of this steam and energy into her work
inside the house. She turned moanful and dreary, heavy
and sad, when she had been over the room a hundred, two
hundred times with fingers and eyes, and there was nothing else to work at. Her white skin, blond hair, pale blue
eyes, and full lips shook like shadows on the cliffs of the
Cap Rock. Tike and Ella May both sat up on the bed and

greeted her as she put the gunnysack in place under the door and heaved the weight of her shoulder against the door to shut it against the wind.

"Wahoo!" Tike held both arms above his head and kicked his feet together above the bed. "Wahooo! God Almight an' little cottontail rabbits, Blanche! God! I'm glad to see you! I'm just about th' gladdest that any man ever was to ever see any womern! Whew! Come in! Blow in! Watch out there! Your clothes are blowin' plumb off!"

"Tiiike," Ella May scolded him in his ear. "Don't tease the poor girl. Shut your mouth." And she smiled as she saw how red Blanche's face was where her hat and her coat did not cover. "Gee. You must just be simply froze, girl. Here. Let me help you to get your coat off."

By this time Blanche had got her wind well enough to point to Ella May and say, "No no no no no no. You just stay right where you are seated. I'll do my own job of getting my things off."

"I'll help." Tike jumped to the floor. "Always did sorta get a big kick outta helpin' a lady to get her 'er clothes off." His eyes burned like signal lights, or like the headlights of a fast car cutting through the dark of the plains at night.

"Tiikke." Ella May dropped her eyes and looked at him. "Don't insult the lady. You might run her off."

"Naw. Just about ever' womern I ever did see got a big bang outta gettin' their clothes took off. Is that right, Blanche?" He tossed her coat onto the back of the cane-bottom chair. He took her wool stocking cap and stuck it down into the pocket of her coat. Blanche looked away from him for a bit, then she turned toward him, determined not to let him get the best of her. There was so much red on her cheeks from the bite of the outside wind that Tike could not tell how much she was blushing. She shook her head as she took a hairnet off, then whipped her hair through the air to shake the cold out of it. Her eyes shot straight into Tike's as she shook her shoulders and arms and rubbed her neck with her hands. And she told him, "Yes. I suppose that most women like to have their clothes took off, but it must be by the right man. And let me give you to understand, Mister Hamlin, that I have undressed a lot more men than you have women. I went to one of the best nurses' colleges in Amarillo for three years. You couldn't show me anything that I didn't see there already. So don't get it into your head that I get all upset at the sight of naked skin."

"What are you blushin' so red about, then?" he teased her. "Look at your face. You're so beat right now that you don't know which end is up! Look!"

"My face is red because of the wind, and not you. And even if I am blushing some, then it is only because I'm blushing for your ignorance."

"My what?"

"Ignorance."

Then Ella May laughed on the bed and clapped her hands together in her lap. "Go to him, Blanche! Go to him! Eat him up and spit him out alive! He thinks that he can embarrass every female that walks before his eyes! Tell him! Get him told! It'll do him good! Ha ha!"

Tike looked from one face to the other, then cracked a dry little bashful grin. "Two onto one! Devil's fun!" His fingers scratched the dandruff at the roots of his hair. "Bunchin' up on me! Bunchin' up!

"I'm one. I'm one you'll not get the goat of." Blanche winked one eye at Ella past Tike's arm. She stood in the middle of the floor with her hands on her hips and imitated a bent, cripply ranch boss or a tobacco-chewing foreman. She moved the end of her tongue around the inside of her cheeks, let her body sway from side to side, eyed Tike up and down, and said, "You think that because I am a young girl that I'm an ignorant girl. You think that because I have no man around that I am all off my nut. You think that I am lonesome. You think that you can get my brain all rattled just by merely mentioning something naked. You have said all kinds of things to me in the ten days I'm here to try and embarrass me. I don't get mad at you even. The men in the hospitals have already said everything to me that you can say, and I don't get mad at them, either. I don't care if they want to undress me and pull me into bed with them ten times a day, I know it is not the men who is to blame. And I know every reason why you say to me what you say, like this, like that, like this and like that. I am a very young and pretty girl and you would give your left arm to lay with me in the hay. I take it as a compliment to me."

"Ha ha ha ha ha ha. Now! There you go! There's your way out! Mister Lady Killer! Ha ha ha ha." Ella May doubled over with sharp pains, and felt like she should not really be laughing so hard. But the look on Tike's face as he stood there with one hand in his hair and the other one down in his pocket was the funniest sight that she had ever seen in her thirty-three years of living. "Whooo whoo whoo whoo. Your train is about to leave on track number nine. You'll have to run fast to catch it!"

Tike was not sore or angry. Yet he pulled his face full of worried wrinkles and took out his sack of tobacco. As he blew a cigarette paper loose and rolled the smoke between his thumb and fingers, he acted like the maddest man that ever set foot on the plains. "Women. Runnin' aroun' readin' books. Loose-footin' it off to all kindsa schools. Sneakin' off to colleges fulla naked men."

"I did not say that the college was filled with naked men." Blanche winked her eye again at Ella May, then drew her face into a deep seriousness.

"You posotutely did, too!" Tike said.

"I absotively did not." Blanche removed her coat and cap from the back of the chair and hung them on a nail in the wall. "Did not."

"Ella May. Lady, you heard her! Didn't she say that she took all th' clothes offa ever' man in that there whole college?" He asked Ella May for her support by holding his hands out toward her like a sweating lawyer. "Huh?"

Ella May disagreed. She shook her head from side to

side as she said, "She said that she took care of all kinds of sick people, men, women, and children, as a part of her hospital training. Not the people that came to the college. Furthermore, she threw you for a twenty-yard loss, Mister Hamlin. You tried your best to embarrass her and you done everything that you could do to hurt her feelings. And then she knocked your props out from under you that she had undressed more men than you have women! Woooheee! Somebody finally did come along to stop old Tike Hamlin's clock! She put a stop to your old dog's barking! Ha ha ha ha!"

"What if ever' shemale womern was to go a-sneakin' off an' go to one of them colleges like that?" He lit his cigarette and felt the nicotine of the smoke sting and bite the lids of his eyes. "What'd it be like to try to live with one of 'em after'ards? Her head'd be so soaked fulla highfalutin notions that they just wouldn't be no livin' amongst 'em. Have no fun outta one."

Blanche started to move to the middle of the floor, but saw that Ella May was about to say something more. She leaned against the rail of the stairs that led up to the roost that had been Tike's sleeping place since Blanche had been with them. She smelled the smoke from his cigarette and the filthy dust from the whole room, and her nostrils moved on her pained face.

"Fun out of one," Ella May spoke out in very certain words. "Fun out of one. Those four little words show you just about your whole way of feeling toward a woman.

Fun out of one. If it's only by digging at her, poking at her, scratching at her, trying your very best to make her feel hurt and bad and embarrassed, making her feel silly, if this is the only way that you can ever have dealings with any woman, then it is a lot better for you not to have any dealings at all. Fun out of one! Did it ever cross your mind, Mister, to have fun with a woman instead of at her? With? Instead of at? Ohhh. I don't intend to say that you are entirely crazy, Tike, because no matter what you say to me, I know how to pass it off, or how to take it, but you have just simply got to get it knocked into your head that you just cannot, cannot, cannot treat every strange lady that you meet this mean and ornery way. What's more, I am really glad that Blanche did cut your water off just like she did just now. It is a lot better to have it happen right here and right now than to have it cause you, and all of the rest of us, lots more pains and troubles somewhere later on."

Tike's temper rose as he listened to her speak. He had not been entirely serious in teasing Blanche. He had done it simply to try to put a little sexy fun into the whole situation. He was not really against women reading books, going to school, college, all they wanted to. But his temper was rising because neither Blanche nor Ella May could see that he was just fooling. This was the thing that caused him to fry and boil. And there was a streak of hot pride somewhere in him that would not allow his lips to say, "I was just foolin'," nor to explain the whole thing. This was one of Tike's worst faults and failings. He said things when he was clowning that he did not mean, and acted his part out so well that people really thought he was serious. One word would lead to another, there would be an argument, and he would not even take one step to cross a hairline and apologize, nor say that he was just kidding.

And Ella May had known him better than anybody else, except for his mama and papa and his two sisters, so she overlooked and forgot these things that other people around Tike kept on holding against him. He had serious disagreements with many of Ella's close relatives, friends, and visitors. She forgot. Others went on remembering. Tike felt a sort of pride about it because it proved that he was such a good actor that he could put it over on people. Most people held it against him, thinking that he would have many more friends to help him if he could only learn to say, "I apologize," "I was only fooling." This streak of "acting" Tike had picked up and learned from his folks all over the place, but when anybody did not quite understand if he was serious or being foolish, then his main feeling was that he only shook his head and said, "Hell with 'em."

Blanche walked across the linoleum floor with her head down, actually waiting for Tike to smile and say that he was only kidding, that he knew better, that he was aware of the fact that the people in her college did not come to class naked, that it was a good thing for the ladies to go to school and to learn, and that he really did not want to hurt her feelings because she did not have a man around. Every step, she waited for him to speak. But Ella May watched and shook her head because she knew that Tike would not speak up. One word from him would cause Blanche to think he was a very wise man instead of an idiot. The word did not come. And Ella May felt the stabs of pain in her stomach and back because Blanche was forced to lick her lips with her tongue and think, "Go ahead, idiot, be an idiot. Live an idiot and die an idiot."

Tike sat down on the first step of the stairs and smoked his cigarette. His head was down, then up, then he gazed out over the room, then his eyes followed all of the humps and cracks in his wallpaper, then they counted the worn-out spots down across the linoleum, and then he gazed and stared out the window and into the ice of the night.

"How is your little lodger?" Blanche asked Ella May. She stood on the floor at the bedside for a time, looking down. She touched her hand to Ella May's forehead, then lifted her hand and counted the beat of her pulse. Her eyes were full of thoughts as she sat down on the bed quilt near Ella's feet. "Any new pains?"

"Little ones. Yes."

"What is the feeling like?"

"Just like everything in the whole world was pushing down on me so hard that I, just, ahhh, I just can't hardly get my breath. Do you know what I mean?"

"Yes. It's, well, you see, it's some of your organs and tissues pushing their way down into position so that they can do their part in the actual delivery," Blanche said.

"It feels like a big dust cloud pushing down against the

ground. It's a cramp. Short of wind. Some sharp little pains like muscles stretched. Then, of course, all of the feeling of bearing down. Pulling down. But really this feeling is getting so low down in me now that it feels like a sort of a relief, I mean it feels better than I had been feeling for some time. Why is this?"

"When the baby is high up inside you it does cause more discomfort than it does after it falls lower. The upper pains are gone. The lower pains are on. That is all."

"Upper plains is gone." Tike gazed steadier out of his window. Held his head high and his knee between his hands. His back was as straight and stiff as Ella's ironing board. "Where they gone off to?"

"She said pains, not plains."

Blanche listened.

"That there dagnabbed wind can blow its firebox out an' blow its self smack smooth to death, but it never could blow these upper plains down onto them lower ones." A dry snap cracked in his words. His eyes wore holes in the window glass as he watched the night get colder and blacker.

"She was telling me about the baby getting down to the lower pains. Shut up. Keep your peepers trimmed out at that window there and keep your yap trap out of our conversation if you just simply will not and cannot act the least bit sensible. Go ahead, Blanche, what were you about to say before the alligators starting bawling over across the holler there?"

Tike made no move to reply. His eyes were still out the

window. He felt his body turn hotter and hotter, like there was too much heat in the room. He looked about the room for some kind of job to fill his itching hands, something that would carry him twenty miles away from this shack and everybody in it. He walked across the floor and opened back the iron door of the heater, looked through its mouth and into its belly full of red-hot blackish coals. As he felt the heat against his lips he licked them damp with his tongue, then shook the coal bucket against the door so loud that the rattle and the noise drowned out the sounds of the women talking, and carried him off down away somewhere into a world of his own along the shale cliffs and the wash canyons of the Cap Rock. He closed the stove door with another loud rattle and then walked seventeen miles across the floor till he come to the wash bench, the buckets, the cans of milk and cream. He stirred among them in a noisy manner, and lifted the big aluminum bowl into its place on the separator. He poured milk into it and then turned the handle, watched the disks till they whirled around at the speed of a thousand times a minute. The steady buzz of the hum of the machine bathed his feelings in the sweetest of waters, set up an orchestra in the halls of his soul, and his creative mind drove a dozen tractors and pulled a thousand plows as he hardened his muscles, and squeezed the wood handle of the crank. The hum was born as a yowling baby in the wheels and the cogs of the machine, and he saw it grow up larger and louder, as large as the whole room and as loud as, then a good bit louder than, the voices of Blanche and Ella May. His face was a sweet bitter mean smile.

Ella May felt a good bit lighter inside as she heard the separator get to whizzing because she knew that the noise would sweep Tike's thoughts and his terrible pride away into the sound of the machine. They could just go on with their talking and forget him for a while. So the crying of the separator was like a singing in the soul, for the baby could breathe better when Ella's belly muscles were not drawn down so hard and so tight. And so for the baby, the singing bowl of the cream machine was like a worldwide symphony played with the four winds against the strings of smoke, against the holes of smokestacks, against the rosin on leaves and bark.

In the whirl of the separator, Tike kept quiet and let his brain roam on the plains. Ella whispered to Blanche on the side of the bed, "Did you ask old man Ridgewood what I told you?"

"You mean about the one acre of land?" Blanche talked so low that Tike could not hear.

"Yes," Ella said.

"I told him which acre you wanted to buy. I drew it off for him on a sheet of paper. I said, like this, the acre just to the north of this house. Was that right?"

Ella shook her head yes. She glanced at Tike's hand on the crank of the separator, then lowered her eyes and her voice again. "Yes."

"He said that I talked like a rabbit in a trash pile. He said that he was going to keep all of his land together. He didn't intend to break it up. I even went so far as to tell him that you folks wanted to dig a cellar on it and put up a house. Then he asked me what sort of house, and I said, Oh, a house, I think, built out of earth of some kind. Then he turned cold all of a sudden and said, absolutely no."

"Absolutely no."

"That is what his words were. Absolutely no."

Ella May felt a dizzy pain all over her body caused by the muscles as they drew tight around her baby. All that she said was, "Ahh. Yes. I see."

Blanche tried to speak a bit sunnier when she saw how dark Ella May's face had turned. "But he said, 'However, you'll find me to be just like another businessman. If you want to build a house out of rocks or dirt or whatnot, I will sell you an acre back here on this outer edge of my wheat land.' And he said, 'That spot of ground that that old wooden house, meaning this one, could be producing wheat, and I intend to tear it down before the year is out.' "

"Do you remember which acre he said he would sell?" Ella asked.

"He said, Anywhere down along the Cap Rock."

"Anywhere? Cap Rock? Oh. Great Jee horsie face! Why, that old rocky stuff wouldn't grow toothpicks. What on earth does he think we are, anyway, that old bloater?" She felt the taste of sorrow on her tongue, and the skin of her knees, arms, elbows, crawled like a snakeskin against a weed. She leaned closer to Blanche with red eyes and hot tears, pulled at the loose yarn on the bed quilt. "How much did he say?"

"Two fifty." Blanche felt her own nose burn and sting. "Said you could not hope to own an acre of this wheat-growing land for less than five, six, eight hundred. And where would you get that?"

Blanche's hair moved in the lamplight as she held her face down and shook her head from side to side. "No. I know," Ella May said. She sent quick glances across the room toward Tike. She heard him rattle the cream cans, buckets, funnels, containers, with one hand as he refilled the big bowl on top of the separator. She felt that Tike had heard their words, but that he made as much noise as he could just to act as if he did not care what they talked about. She saw his muscles move and roll as he turned the crank and lifted cans. She felt that he tried very hard to make so much noise that he would drown out their conversation. She lifted her voice and spoke louder to see if he would rattle his cans louder. Instead of this, as her words came into his, Tike turned the crank at its fastest speed and sang an old song:

Well, they don't grow no more cane along the river!
No, the cutting plow don't run here any more!
But this dirt had oughta be mighty rich, boys,
There's a man dead in the middle of each row!

She had heard him sing the song a hundred times before, and he had told her that a Negro chuck wagon cook from Louisiana had sang it for him and had taught it to five or six of the cowmen. His voice sang in a sour chant, long, wailing, and his words floated out through his nose. He sang to make the two women think that he did not care what they talked about in such low words. But Tike had lied to his own self, because as he sang he would have given his last dollar to hear their words.

A few days ago, when Blanche had spent her fourth day with the Hamlins, Ella May had told her about Tike's craving to get out of the old wooden house and to raise up a house of earth. How she had read and read again the pages of the little book from the Department of Agriculture, and how he had worn it thin in his pockets. Not once, not even once, since that book had come in the box had Tike let it get away from him, except to pass it from his own hands to hers. The little book had always been warm with the heat of his hands, the warmth of his pocket, smeared and soaked with his sweat and hers.

Her old daddy had paid her one dollar a day for keeping his lands and accounts in order during her last year at home. He had given her a check written out for "Three Hundred and Sixty Five and No/100 Dollars" several months before she married Tike. Tike had almost caught her several times when she seemed to get money right out of thin air, a few dollars to pay their fuel bill at the co-op filling station on Highway 66. He had been very angry about it several times, accused her of borrowing money from her daddy, but she figured with a pencil and paper and proved to him every time that she had simply kept a penny here, a nickel here, a dollar here, one yonder, and had hidden the bills away until they "amounted up." In this way she had spent about one hundred and sixty-some dollars, which left in the Citizens' State Bank two hundred and one, two, or three dollars, she did not know exactly. But Tike had never found it out. If she had explained the whole thing to him on the day they were married, he would have smiled and passed it off with a joke, but she had made the mistake of trying to surprise him with it later, and if she told him now, he would not believe it. There would be one wild man running loose around there for no less than a week or ten days. He would ask, "If ya earned it right an' honest offa yer old daddy, then how come ya kept it hid out alla this time?"

To keep him from having such fits, she made matters worse by keeping her bank account a Q.T. secret.

Three or four times during the last year she had started to go into Ridgewood's office to see about buying one acre of land. She had decided on the acre to the north of the house because they could live in the wood shack and build up the earth one at the same time, time would be saved in going to and from the job, there would be water, tea, coffee to drink, and meals could be fixed on the oil stove. The farm chores had to be done, and the earth house should be as close as possible. Three or four times it had crossed her mind to walk into Ridgewood's office and see about it. She could get an idea of how much he wanted, make her down payment, come home with her deed of ownership, which would make Tike glad because she was pregnant and the birth was coming on. And yet she had not gone in to see Ridgewood. Every time she had been in town her feet had started and then stopped, turned some other way.

The last three or four weeks she had been afraid to take the trip into town. And now the baby was due to be born at any minute. Tike would have no more allowed her to go than he would have laid his head down across their chopping block and had somebody cut it off. And so she had told Blanche to go see Ridgewood. And tonight Blanche had told her what he had said. "I don't bust up my land. You talk like a crazy woman."

Ella May held her hand over her left breast as the hurt tightened in her body. She felt the small knot that had come just above her breast that day a year ago that Tike's elbow had bruised her. She leaned her head over Blanche's lap as the muscles drew tighter and the pain worse. The skin under her hand was hot enough to sweat through her dress and onto the palm of her hand. She had not told Blanche. She had not told Tike. She had noticed it a bit every day. She felt the small knot of muscle, no larger than the rubber on a lead pencil, situated barely under skin about an inch above the bulge of her breast. She had said to herself, but never out loud, "Everybody has enough pains of their own without me adding any more onto them." Then on other days when she was sure that somebody had noticed her, she had thought that she would just come right out with the whole story and see if it was a serious bruise. And then again she had said under her breath, "Oh, it is such a little spot, such a teensy-weensy little old spot, that I just know it can't stay for long. Why, I've had ten times worse knocks than that and the bruise has always gone away." Then, right here lately, the thing seemed to hurt her sharper on account of the way that the baby in her stomach pulled down on the muscles of her ribs and shoulders. And here of late she had been a lot more scared about it, because she actually caught herself thinking about it for longer stretches of time. And why she did not break down and let anybody else know was more than she could explain.

Just a little bruise. Such a little spot. No bigger than a good-size wart on a log. No bigger than a titty on a hog. No bigger, not much bigger than the head of a knitting needle, not much bigger than a small green pea, not near as big as the head on a dime. This spot. This one little teensy-weensy spot. Why did she not tell anybody? Why?

She did not know. But it would be better. When the baby gets out and the weight gets off my stomach, she thought, then these aches and pains in all of my muscles will quit and go away. My calves and my feet and my ankles hurt too, but so do my hips and my groin and so do my eyes and my shoulders and my back. It's just because the baby is pulling down on me from all over. When I straighten up it's not quite so miserable, but then it's just almost more than I can do to sit up straight all of the time. Such a little spot. Little old spot's not as big as I am. I'll lick it and I'll whip it and I'll give it a good beating and make it go away.

"Go away, spot. Go, go, away. Go somewhere and get in somebody like old landlord Ridgewood." She would say a thousand such things to herself at night in bed, all day at her work, her bending, her lifting, walking.

And so as Blanche told her that Ridgewood would sell only the one acre of land over near the Cap Rock, Ella May saw the lamplight and the room whirl in front of her. She saw her life and her world and all of her people spin before her, and inside her brain there was such a foam and such a splash that she could not control her thoughts.

Blanche had not been able to see Ella May's face as she leaned over her, and the rattle and the bang of Tike's work, the humming and moaning of the cream separator, had got louder than ever. Blanche held her hand flat against Ella May's back to brace her a bit in her humped position.

"Feel any pains, Mrs. Hamlin?" Blanche said close to her ear.

And Ella shook her head as her hair fell in long strings down past her eyes. She was crying, sniffling, yet Tike could not hear, nor Blanche either.

"Any pains?" Blanche repeated. A strong soapy clean smell was in Ella May's hair. Blanche held her by the arms and spoke louder, "If you feel any pains, Mrs. Hamlin, you tell me!"

Ella May, instead of saying anything, bit her bottom lip again until it turned blue and black and her forehead and face wrinkled like little dunes of sand that sifted in and settled at several places on the linoleum. She tossed her head and shoulders from side to side and Blanche heard the sounds of her sobbing, but it was not until Blanche's eyes fell down onto Ella's clenched hand on the quilt that Blanche saw the full torture that was in Ella May's body. Ella's blood veins stood out like dark vines against a tree, and her hands clawed into the covers like dry roots reaching for water. "No, no, no, no," was the only thing that Ella spoke, and this in a hush and a whisper of misery between her teeth.

"Is it bearing down? Tell me? I can't help you unless you talk to me. Tell me. Tell me. Talk. Talk to me." For a short time Blanche tried to hold on to her arms by wrestling with her on the bed, then she saw that the covers were all being twisted, and that blue marks were forming on Ella's arms. She let go and rose up onto her feet. She took two or three steps backward in order to get a good look at Ella and to study the nature of the pains.

Ella May's stomach moved up and down. Blanche waited to see if the movement was caused by crying or the crying was caused by the movement. Was her heavy breathing making the baby rise and fall or was the rise and fall of the baby the cause of her heavy breathing? Under the loose cotton dress, to the eye of Blanche, all of the motion of her stomach was well known, but the dimness of the lamp and the shadows of the wrinkles on Ella's dress caused Blanche to have to look a bit closer. She tried with all her skill not to upset Ella nor Tike any worse than need be.

Ella stood with her feet apart on the floor. She put forth all of her strength in order to stand up tall and straight with her face high to the ceiling. And it was the sting of the pain of her bruise above her breast that caused her to let her shoulders fall limber. Her leather work shoes were loose at the ankles, their strings untied dragged around her feet on the floor. Two lightweight pairs of cotton socks of a speckled gray color were enough to keep out the bite of the frost in the wind. And as her shoe soles, which were cut from old truck tires, moved on the linoleum, she stood in her tracks and turned around and around. Her lifted eyes were in the light, the hollows across her face were the same as the shadows of the new-plowed land in the light of the moon. Her dress was not a thing of rags and tatters because Ella May Hamlin would have let you find her dead on the ground before she would have let you catch her in a rotten, holey dress. A few of her good things had gone rotten and got torn to pieces, but they were now rags in her mop, Tike's grease rags for his machinery, or else they had been pushed and punched into the cracks in the walls and floors to keep out the weather. She turned around as slow as a cloud drifting, her eyes saw the room and the things in the room but saw, too, on through the walls and out into the lash and the whip of a fast blizzardy wind.

She seemed to be a frozen icicle, a loose shingle, some kind of a windmill turning about. She did not turn in complete circles, but only in a half circle, then halfway back around, then the other direction for three-fourths of a turn, and it seemed that forces inside her fought to push her first one way around, then the other. She did not get to finish a turn because another rush of thoughts, feelings, old-time memories, new plans would rip across her, spin her back around, and the expressions on her face changed in the light and shadows as often as more mixtures of feelings took control of her. She held her hands opened wide apart, down at her sides, and she muttered words such as, "I've come this way. Come this way and this is me. Ha ha ha. Yes. This is the little girl you knew. Ha ha. Yes, yes. This is me. This is me here. This is me walking all up and down. Am I not a pretty girl to see? I saw my pretty time and I saw myself in my own looking glass, and I looked and I said, there you are. I know that is you. Ohhh. Yes. That is you. And so now this is me here. Me here walking. Me talking. Almost everybody said that I was the prettiest little lady on the whole upper plains. I guess I was. I must have been. I could have been. It was either me or that Beverly Judison, and I'm sure and certain that it wasn't her. It was me. Me. It is still me. If you please, if you please sir, this is me."

The words were spoken in time and rhythm with the sway of her body and legs. She seemed to flirt with the bed, wink at the stove, make eyes at the walls and at the papers, and at her bale, the oil stove, the wash bench, the water bucket, the dipper, then at Tike and his separator cans. It was when she bowed and spoke to Blanche that Blanche tried to get a straight look into her eyes. Ella let her gaze fall down across the floor and did not let Blanche see her straight. Blanche watched her closer than ever to see if she was dancing in delirious pain or merely having fun.

From the east, north, west, and south, Ella took in the strength for the baby inside her, she inhaled her lungs deep and full of the electricity in the room. Like a ship, she charged her own power into her own batteries. Her words had the same sound as a squeaky windmill.

Blanche had seen other women do things like this, things a little bit delirious, in order to gain some kind of strength to let a new baby come into the world. She was not nervous, nor frightened, just cautious, making sure and certain. Buckets of clean water were on the bench, a small suitcase filled with newspapers, strips of cloth, clean washrags. Why worry? The night outside was howling a blizzard, the wind pushing down across the plains harder than a hurricane on the ocean, because the sea rises and falls and forms into waves that are like mountains and valleys to check, slow, and break the wind. The flat lands of the plains were as level as the old linoleum on the floor, and there was nothing to stop the wind for fifteen hundred miles to the north, nothing except a small gully, a canyon, a town, a barbed-wire fence, the house of a landowner, the shack of a renter or sharecropper, and these things did not stop nor hinder that icy wind any more than a wild bull would be stopped by a rabbit track.

It was with all of this in the back of her mind that Blanche watched and studied Ella's funny little dance.

Blanche waited until Ella May had moved to the center of the floor. Then she fixed the pillow, turned the covers down, and said, "You had best come and lay yourself down here in this bed. Let me take care of you for a while. I think you are getting ready for your big push. Come on." She talked with her back to Ella May, and when she waited for her to reply, there was nothing except Tike's chanting and the whine of the whirling disks in the separator. She patted her hands on the pillows and covers and said again, "Do you not think that it is time for you to stretch your bones out and give that little monkey some rest?" And there was still no reply.

There was only Tike singing, the separator humming. Blanche silent and waiting, touching her fingers to the bed. And this was only for a few short seconds.

But in these few short seconds Ella May took a woolly brown shawl from a nail on the wall, threw it around her shoulders, hugged her stomach in her hands, and walked across the floor to the door. With each step she gritted her teeth and spoke with a hiss of a snake, "No. No no. No. No no no." Her right hand held the weight of her stomach and her left hand took hold of the doorknob. She swallowed hard to try to keep down the thousand miseries that were eating at her. As her hand turned the knob she saw a vision, a picture before her of several million people all going and coming in and through and inside one another. It was a message, she thought, and as she thought, the vision came clearer, and she heard words that said, "Here are the people in this room going and coming. They go and they come in and through, in and through one another. And the people of the farms and the ranches around, they go and they come in and through, in and through one another. Like the weeds, the stems, the hay, straws and lints, like the powders, chalks, dusts arise and fall and pass in and through, in and through one another in the winds, the sun. And the people are all born from one and they are really all one. The people are all one, like you and your baby are one, like you and your husband, both of you are one. And all of the upper north plains are one big body being born and reborn in and through one another, and those also of the lower south plains. All of those of the Cap Rock. This is the greatest one single truth of life and takes in all other books of knowing. This is the only one truth of life that takes in all of the other works. And there are a few people that work to hurt, to hold down, to deny, to take from, to cheat, the rest of us. And these few are the thieves of the body, the germs of the disease of greed, they are few but they are loud and strong and your baby must be born well to help kill these few out."

And nobody in the little room heard these words except Ella May. And she did not hear these words in these very words, but in words that showed her even plainer, much plainer, what her vision had meant. Her vision showed her that all of the people live and move in and through each other exactly like her baby lived and moved in and through her. And all of the words that she would hear in her life would make the picture plainer.

The frost in the wind of the open door bit Tike on the skin like a little sheepherding dog, and it chewed at Blanche's ankles and caused her to stomp her feet. She chilled up and down the back, her hands drew up in front of her face like claws of the eagle, and for a short space of time it seemed that her entire life and soul flew out at her open mouth. And she whirled, spun around on her heel, and felt the waves of the wind hit her full in the face and chest. She ran her gaze around the room, up the little staircase to the roost, then at the separator, Tike, and all of the buckets and cans. He felt the blizzard wind at the back of his sweaty shirt, but it took him a few short seconds to get his mind to register what was going on. The separator hummed, and he sang his chant:

Another man done gone
Another man done gone
Another man done gone
Another man done gone

Well I did not know his name
Well I did not know his name
No I did not know his name
And I did not know his name

"Ella Mayyy!"

He killed another man
ʒumm ʒumm ʒumm ʒumm
He killed another man
Sum summmm ʒummm sum
He killed another man
And he killed

"Tike!"

He had a long chain on
He had a long
Huh?

"Ella May! God!"

"Ella what?" The sound of the separator died down slowly and by its own accord, because of the heavy weight of the steel disk cups that turned at a thousand revolutions a minute. His back was in a tired hunch as he turned about and blinked his eyes at Blanche. "Who?" Before Blanche could make a motion or sound, Tike felt the cold from the open door, and he dived out into the night. "Lady." He made an attempt to open his mouth but the zero blizzard took his breath away so fast that he could not do any more than sort of bark, "Lady, Lady, where are you at? Holler. Where 'bouts are ya at? Hey. Lady." And then he turned his mouth a bit out of the wind and said louder, "LADY!" And then he growled in a madder tone, "Th' good God Jesus oughta take it outa yore ole sore hide f'r pullin' a trick like this! LADY!"

Blanche stepped across the room to take her coat off the wall, but the small strap hung on the nail, and she ripped a long narrow hole from the collar down the back, and after three hard pulls, she flung the coat against the wall, covered her chest with her bare hands and ran out in the storm at Tike's back. "She over there? Whew. This wind cuts through your skin like a branding iron! See her?"

"Naw." Tike's voice came out of the sheets of dark and wind. "Naw. That ain't her. That's th' water tank. Lady never did pull no such of a monkeyshine as this before since I knowed 'er. LADY. LADY! Talk up!"

"What is that over there?"

"Where 'bouts?"

"There." Blanche felt her finger freeze as stiff as a stove poker when she took it away from her warm neck to point. "Right there. There on the ground?"

"Ohhh. Yeahhhh. Thank Jesus. Lady, now, honey, mommy, Lady, will you just tell me why in the hell you jumped up and pulled any such a caper as this? Was it on accounta that I'm so no good to ya? Here. Git up. Blanche, help me? Lord Jesus, Lady, you ain't got th' stren'th in ya to stand no such a damn blizzard as this is."

And the open door of the little room allowed the wind to chase in like a whole stockyard of animals drunk on silo juice. Like the mean and greedy spirits of ten hundred nickel-begging saints fighting to enter into the little body of the baby, to be born again here tonight, to preach, to beg, to bum dimes to get drunker on. And all of these wayward souls flew straight into the glass globe of the coal oil lamp on the eating table. And the claws of the night demons reached to steal the flame of the fire because they thought that it was the soul of all life, the warmer of all bodies, the strength in all action. The fire in the lamp globe had higher ideas and craved to light the way for the baby to be born, craved, too, just at the right instant, to melt out into the air of the room at the moment that the baby took its first breath, and to be inhaled, sucked in, drawn into the lungs and the blood, the brain and the eyes, the soul of the lamp fire fought the unborn blizzard spirits because if they devoured its flame before it could be breathed into the nose of the baby, then it would take several million years again to get to be a flame of fire again, a flame struck and placed there by the hand of a woman with a baby in her stomach. The room shook, trembled, splashed and foamed, rolled and tossed, pitched and squirmed, with the shadows of the battle that was going on between the flame or fire and the outer winds down inside the lamp globe. The winds howled into all of the private corners of the room, sniffled, smelled, prodded, felt with their deathly fingers, and danced with such a wild passion that they nearly succeeded in stealing the lamplight. The things about the room flashed light and dark like the gunfire from the muzzles of a million freedom cannons.

And the voices of Tike and Blanche lifting, working,

scolding, and coaxing Ella May, these voices drifted into the room and all through the walls and the floor, the ceiling, the stairs, and up in the attic to the roost.

"Kill yer own self an' yer baby like this."

"And kill both of us with the pneumonia."

"What did ya ever do it for? Say? Talk? Hold her up by her feet. I got her hands. Talk? Lady?" There was a tender roughness in Tike's voice. "Talk? Lady?"

And Blanche said, "If your baby lives through this, then it will live through everything." She pushed her way in at the door with one of Ella's feet in each hand. "Why did you ever do such a thing?"

Tike carried her head and shoulders with a hand under each arm. Tike was not a man to get afraid of anything very easily, no matter how big, how little, how ugly, how mean, it was. This was the worst three minutes that he had ever lived through so far. His blood had left his face a dusty white, and the chill of the wind had set his face like a rock and his eyes like marble stones.

Ella had been easy to handle so far. The stingers in the whip of that wind had not really dealt her much bodily damage outside the shock of the thing. She had been easy to carry, but just as she felt Blanche carry her feet through the door she twisted, turned, and set up a nervous fit of kicking. "No. No. No," were the only words she would speak. It took all of Tike's strength to lift her past the door and to kick it shut behind him. And while they forced her over onto the bed, she screamed out louder, "No NO NOOO!"

The wind knocked the door open again at Tike's back. He kicked it shut with such a bang that the draft of air blew the lamp out.

"See what you have done," Blanche spoke out in the dark when she sat down on Ella May's bed to keep her from tossing herself onto the floor. "See? Be still."

"Ya got us all so dadblamed scared that th' light's jumped clean outta th' lamp globe. Why'ncha talk? Make some sense? Darkest dern dark I ever seen in all of my put togethers. Cut it with a knife." Tike felt about in the room for the orange crate just above the eating table and Blanche sighed with relief when he rattled his fingers in the matchbox. "Matches. There. Whooapp. Dropped 'em. God blame it all ta th' devil nohow. Lady. Look what'cha made me do. Talk up. Come ya ta pull any such a stunt anyway?"

And it was there in the dark that Ella May rolled on the bed and cried into the covers, "Everything made me do it. I don't know."

There was no shaft, no flicker, no hint of light in the room. The darkness outside joined with the darkness inside and while Tike felt on the tablecloth for the matches that he had dropped, it seemed that for a while the cold and the blizzard and the darkness had won out against his hand, there, hunting for his match.

"See what a bad place th' farm would be, Lady, if th' dark was ta blow th' sun out?"

"Strike a match," Blanche told Tike.

"Light," Ella said.

"Be no light in this here house till ya tell me why it was that ya done what ya done. Blizzard."

And Ella answered there in the dark, "I, I just simply couldn't, I couldn't stand the thought of my baby being born here in this old stink pot of a shack. It wasn't me, Tike, it wasn't me. I had but little to do with it. You must, you must believe this. I am the gladdest woman on these old tumble-weed plains tonight because my baby is your baby, and because we have come this far without letting my old landhog daddy give us any help. And me, me, I, ah, oh, I don't care for my own self, my own comfort, really, Tike, you must see this. I don't know any more why I put on that little friz-zledy shawl and ran off out into that blizzard, I don't know why. I never will know why. I saw something in my mind, something like a lot of pictures, all run and melted together, ah, something about people all mixed up with each other. I saw how my finger puts a seed down in the ground and I saw how that was hitched up, or tied up somehow, with a lady at a desk somewhere, a family packing tobacco into a barn, men riding on a ship somewhere. I saw exactly how their work traced back to me and mine to them. And then I looked at this room here and this whole house and I didn't see a house, but I saw some kind of a big big big trap worse than a big big big steel trap or a net. And the trap had long sharp teeth and I saw this whole big trap shut its teeth down around my baby's head and my baby's neck. God. That is all that I remember."

Tike said only, "Well, I be dog."

And Blanche rubbed Ella May's forehead in the dark and said, "I believe that is the strangest nightmare that any patient of mine ever had. Did it seem to have a meaning of any kind?"

"Yes." Ella May spoke with her face burning and her eyes up toward the ceiling. "It did. Did you find the matches, Tike? Hurry up. Light the lamp. This awful dark is pushing down on top of me like a tractor running over me. It makes me see old Dan Platzburgh like I saw him when he cranked his tractor and it was in gear and pushed him over backward and climbed on top of him and the blades on the front wheels cut his two arms off right at the elbows, and the big back wheels stabbed him all through and through with long muddy cleats, and the harrow plow on the back end came along and tore him into a thousand different pieces and scattered him all over our field. And you can't hardly set your foot on an inch of these wheat lands that somebody's meat and bones hasn't been scattered over with. Did you find the box of matches again, Tike?"

Tike had had his fingers on the matchbox where he had dropped it on the table for the past few minutes, but it was under the cover of this dark room that he wanted Ella May to keep talking. Instead of answering her, he simply grunted, muttered under his breath, and tapped his hands about on the tablecloth. "Hmm. Mmm."

"Any bad pains from your dash up the north pole?" Blanche felt Ella's warm hands touch on her own. "Feel all right?"

"Ohhh. I feel all right." Ella's words had the sound of drifting in from some mile-away canyon. "I didn't really fall hard out there in the yard. I just ran a little ways and then the cold wind hit me and it brought me down around to my right senses, it seems. I didn't fall hard. Just kneeled down. Just like a sinner in church. I just prayed. I never did pray before, but I know that I prayed out there in that wind."

"For what?" Blanche asked.

"For some kind of house for my baby. Some house that would keep out all of this dirt and all of this filth and, funny, ha ha ha ha, while I was bent over out there in that wind and those few flickers of fine snow were blowing against my skin, I wasn't to say, what you would call cold. Because, ahhhh, ohhh"—these grunts and strains came with the move of her muscles as she spread her feet apart and rubbed her heels against the sheet—"ahhhh. I was in a house, and it wasn't any old rotten house like this. It wasn't any old windfall, crazy, insane coyote trap like this one. It had walls, walls as thick as this mattress, and rooms just like I marked off on the ground with that stick. Do you remember, Tike?"

"Yeah."

"Did you strike the light yet? Tike?"

"Still huntin'."

And Blanche asked, "Did you two really draw your house plans already so soon?" Her eyes saw all of the junky trash in this room even though the lamp was out and the darkness heavier than blankets. "Already?"

"Just with a stick," Tike told her. "Backyard out there.

Out there just about where she fell down at. Wasn't it, Lady?"

"And I, I, ohhh, mmmmhhhh, I was really inside the house. I felt it. I saw it. And the blizzard ran down like an old locoed cow, and it battered its silly brains out against those walls that we had raised up and the walls were as tough and as hard as the very earth itself and that blizzard, ha ha, just went, *Brrrzzzzzttt*. Fizzled out. Hit my walls and had to turn around me and go on and on and on on on ohhhh."

Blanche said, "Well. What do you know about that?"

And Tike by his table said something that nobody could understand.

"But. But there was something even still lots funnier than that." Ella's whole body moved in a regular rhythm, up, over, and back again, then up and over and back again, and Blanche knew that the first pains of the birth were well under way. And Ella kept on, "I opened my eyes and I saw that the whole house, the house of earth, was papered inside, all over the insides with little books from the Government. Little books that tell you how to build your house, how to dig its cellar and keep it nice and clean and dry, and how to stucco it on the outside so that the wind and the sun can't eat it down. How to paint it and roof it and how to put the windows in it, and how to draw your own plans on your own ground and shape it up with your own hands to fit right into your own dream. And all of these little books were pasted flat up against the walls. Everywhere I look I see them. I see them now. Ohhhhh. Uhhh. Here I am now.

This is me again. Me again walking. Ohhhh ahhh. Ughhh. Tike, strike me a match. I want to see our earth house in the good good good light. I don't want little Tikey Junior the Second to even so much as stick his little head out here in this old messy crazy pukey dark."

Blanche felt the warmth of Ella's face with one hand. With her other hand she touched the leg of Tike's pants in the dark. "I suppose that we had best have some light on this business. Strike your light, Mister Hamlin. I guess that your new house should be well lighted. Was it?"

Tike struck a match against his thumbnail and held it in front of his face while the flame flew upward, then flared its brightest, and then died down to burn along the wood. "Bound to been." He smiled with a deep, serious grin. "Who'd raise up a house outta earth bricks an' then not run it fulla eee-leck-y-triss-eye-teee?" The match flame carried his words out slow and long and floated them up into the air. "Not us by a dam site."

"I saw that too. I saw even the dam site where our electricity was made. I don't know where it was, but it was away off somewhere. A whole ocean of water seemed to be on one end of a wire and it milked our cows, churned our butter, lighted our house, and even swept our floors on this end."

"Ain't a droppa water in ninety mile o' here. An' they ain't no man a livin' can sweep this floor with 'lectricity nohow. An' a six-foot hunk of copper wire would cost twicet as much's this whole blamed house. Ain't nobody gonna build

no wire line o' no kind away out here to this lousy dump."
He lifted the globe and lit the wick of the lamp.

"I think you're right for once in your life." Blanche shook
her head toward Tike. "If you was to nail a copper wire onto
this dilapidated antique, it would all fall down. *Booom*. Just
that way." She fanned her hand in the air to show what she
meant.

Ella May smiled with a sharp pain, moved from side to
side, and said, "But you can nail all of the copper wires you
wish to on my new house of earth. And it will just stand
there and ask for more. And you can just take and hang it
all full of fancy lightbulbs and trinkets and buttons and gad-
gets and springs and triggers and fuses and the henhouse
too, and then the barn to boot, and the cowshed of the earth,
and the big earth wall all around the lot and all around the
barns and around the yards. You can't break them down
with electric wires because they're this thick, and this wide,
and you can run ten tractors right into them and not tear
them down. And you'll live to see this little old measly stink
hole of a dung pile shine out brighter after night than it does
now by day. Ohhhh. Goshhhh. Blanche. Mhhhmmm. I'm
afraid. Afraid that I feel some armies marching around in
my stomach, or else some work gangs building up a power
dam in there. I don't know just. Mmmhhhh. Which." Her
tongue was purple between her teeth as she tried to laugh.
"Tike, you old silly galoot, you, don't you know that there
wasn't a drop of water within three hundred miles of Los

Angeles, but they have got a couple or three lamp bulbs out there that burn on electricity."

"Imitation electricity. Phony. All them lights an' stuff out there in Hollywood's imitation. Buildin's is. Actors is. They couldn't bring us no 'lectric cow juicer. They don't even know we're a livin'."

"No. Not them. But we have got rivers around here that we could dam up and make our own electricity." Ella laughed a bit. "I think I am really going to paper my new earth house with Government books."

"Musta froze your brain up." Tike tried to sound rough and serious, but there was more than a little tenderness and melted snow in his throat. "Froze somethin'. Head ain't a-runnin' right."

"If my head has stopped dead, it still operates much better than that old thing of yours." Ella smiled now with more relief, more comfort, because she felt that Tike was regaining his old self again. She felt worried for a few minutes that he would think that her dash out the door was somehow connected with getting away from him. "If I had been dead ten years and the eagles had picked my bones clean, I could still think better with an empty skull than you do with yours full of sourdough."

"You think them 'lectricity fellers is gonna spend eight thousan' smackeroos ta put a power line two 'er three miles all th' way over ta our place even if it was built with three barns an' two houses an' all made outta Portlan' seement?

Hell no. Ain't 'nuff houses roun' this buffalo waller. Gotta be more houses an' more folks a-livin' out here." He sat back on the edge of the table and ran his finger over the cloth as he frowned down at his shoes. "More."

Ella May lifted her voice into a cry that sounded to Blanche like a real one. She gritted her teeth, shook her head, and squinted her eyes tight and shut. "Well, now, if you aren't a good one! Just stand there and look down at your old mean feet! If you're not just about the meanest and hatefulest and the worst of all the men that I ever had the displeasure of meeting! More people? More houses? Well, Mister Tikeroo Hambone, will you please try to tell me just what you think I am doing here flopped across this bed with this big lump in my stomach, having all of these labor pains and painful labors for?" She had lifted her head and shoulders up a few inches from the pillow but let her weight fall down with force enough to shake the floor under the bed. "Oooo. Will you try to tell me just what you think I'm doing here? Posing for a movie magazine? Ohhhh. Jeeezus."

"Easy." Blanche listened to the whole show with sharp ears.

Ella May was not afraid, but she was frightened that Tike would be. Tike, himself, was not afraid but was only nervous because he feared that Ella May would be afraid.

Blanche had been the one to carry healthy feelings between wife and husband many times before, in her hospital training and in a dozen or so actual births that she had been on. Just how she came to be at the Hamlin shack is a long story that runs through the births of several babies for a hundred miles around. She had all of the papers that a trained nurse needs, yet she was not an actual medical doctor. She could stand in for a doctor but could not replace him. She could perform most of the things that a doctor could perform, yet she was not called a doctor. There was only one expert baby doctor in this entire county, only one who had all of the most modern tools, equipment, and knowledge. There were two others, an old absentminded grouch that might or might not come, and a younger fellow with a black mustache who upset the nerves of his patients by making strange remarks from famous plays and operas. Blanche did not charge a fee of any kind. She heard of a pregnant woman by word of mouth, and simply paid her a visit, had an all-day talk, and as a general rule she stayed a few days or weeks, received her room, board, and whatever sum of money the people paid her. She was very well known and warmly welcomed into any ranch or farmhouse door, yet at the same time, being so pretty, she had many kinds of passionate skirmishes with men. As to her love life, nobody seemed to know anything for certain, and many tales traveled the country both pro and con. She was not what is called a midwife nor a hoodoo healer of any kind. Her full breasts and strong body had caused more than one man to attempt to go to bed with her both indoors and out. Tike Hamlin, feeling a craving for an active sex life, had managed to feel of her body a few times, and burned several hours of each day and night to feel more of her. Of course she was several thoughts ahead of him on this matter, and had never entered into the spirit of the thing with him.

Tike had never in his life learned the unhandy art of keeping his cravings a secret. To him a craving was a craving—he did not make them, so did not have to feel ashamed of them. He had said over and over to Ella May that he would "really like to roll that Blanche in a way that she'd admire."

Ella May felt like she was not in a position to satisfy Tike in her usual way, so if there was a ripple of hurt in her, she more than made up for it by ripples of joy that she was with a child, which to her was the world's greatest work. She did not proceed to even scold Tike for smacking his mouth at the sight of Blanche. She simply told him a dozen times, "It is purely up to you and Blanche, not me." Tike even went to great pains to try and convince Ella that he had been with another woman or two since her pregnancy, but she had always known that he was lying. Over and over, he had asked her if she would get mad at him if he was to roll Blanche in the hay. And over and over Ella had shaken her head and said, "If you feel that you need the practice, go ahead."

And now that the three of them were close together in the one little room, Tike felt all of the joys and hurts that Ella May felt with his baby in her belly. He already felt proud of the new jobs that would come along as the kid grew. He ran here and there, lightened Ella's chores, and did most of her lifting and pulling, yet he could not shake this hot fire out of his brain that flared up as his eyes looked Blanche up and down. It was not the feeling of wanting to go away with her and live the rest of his life, it was just the old craving to touch her, to hold her, to feel her skin, to kiss her, and to bite her all over. He even tried to hold such a feeling down, not to let it come into his mind, but the more that he fought against it, the bigger the thing moved inside him.

Blanche knew that the labor pains of Ella May there on the bed would not bring any relief to Tike's passions. The baby would be there howling and kicking before the morning light, but Tike would keep on feeling this way toward Blanche even after Ella May was up walking around.

"How would you like to have a job, Tike?" Blanche asked. She walked to the wash bench, the stove, the closet, to her suitcase, then filled two large buckets and a teakettle with water and set them on burners to heat. "One that will get you out from under my feet for a few minutes at least?"

"Wish't I was under yore feet. But I ain't."

"Do you want a job? Yes or no."

"Yes."

"Put on your coat and your gloves and go out and get that shovel there against the house, then go down by the cowshed somewhere, there back of it, and dig us a hole."

"Hole." Tike stood for a moment. "Kinda hole?"

"Just a hole. Oh. About the size of a washtub. So deep." Blanche moved so smooth and fast about the room that Tike followed her every step. He watched her like she was some kind of a machine moving.

"Gonna do? Bury 'er?" He moved across the floor, half smiling and half afraid.

Ella May lay on the bed and saw herself in her earth house. She did not hear what had been said. She moaned and sighed in a babylike way to her own self for her own amusement.

"Shh." Blanche took Tike's heavy shirt down from its nail and held it up behind him as he slipped into it. "Shh. Just a little hole big enough to bury the afterbirth in, that's all. Here. Here's your coat. I know it's as cold out there as a blizzard can be, but we have got to get rid of it and we can't leave it out on top of the ground anywhere because the animals will all smell it and get into it."

And then, to keep Ella May from catching on, Tike walked out the door, cursing, "All I got to say is, by God, damn me to hell anyhow, this is one fine time to send me out into th' face of a damned blue blizzard to get just one little lousy bucket of water." He slammed the door, shaking the house all over, and carried his shovel down behind the cowshed.

Ella May and Blanche could hear the dim ringing of Tike's shovel against the hard-frozen topsoil. To Ella it sounded not like a shovel but like the voices of bells, bells of a thousand tones, and the bells had tongues and sang out of their mouths. She saw the bells all over the plains and heard them as they filled the room. They felt the baby push, move down a part of an inch, then push and move down another way. The pain she did not want Tike nor Blanche to see. That needle pain that burned above her left breast she smiled and laughed to hide. Tike down behind that cowshed in this blizzard did not have the least idea that the ring of his shovel was in the room. In her mind, somehow, Ella mixed the sound of the shovel in with the crank of the separator, the rattle of milk buckets. She closed her eyes as her dreams spun past, and talked in a smiling whisper.

Blanche understood a few words but not enough to make any sense out of them. She worked with her cloths, old rags, papers, fixed her two rubber sheets near the head of the bed, speaking to Ella as if she knew every pain, smile, thought. All four of the coal oil burners on the stove were lit and shot whitish, reddish purple lights out through the mica glass doors. Fumes from the newly lit burners mixed in with the steamy vapors from the buckets of water and Blanche felt the sting in her nose. She frowned as she worked and prayed that the fumes would not make it any worse for Ella May. The steamy oil soot became heavier in the air and settled on cobwebs in the high corners where the winds touched easiest. And Blanche worked with a heavy, empty weight in her body, a weight that grew heavier when she looked about the house of rot. She licked her tongue across her lips, then swallowed the saliva in her mouth and tasted the acid burn of the winter dust and oil fumes.

Ella May's lips tasted the poison dust, and she asked, "Where are all those cowbells coming from?"

Blanche set her ears in the direction of Tike's shovel. She worked around the stove, touched a pot, stooped to look in the door of a burner, carried an extra dipper of water from the wash bench to pour into the buckets. Her nose was stubby, shiny, and pink like a slick-skinned cherry. Tears blurred her eyes like hot breath on a cold windowpane. She thought of opening up a window or cracking a door, but knew it would only bring more dirt. The smells from the oil stove made her eyes pink around the rims, and caused her temples to throb and ache. All that she said in reply to Ella May was, "Hmmmm? Bells? Cowbells?"

Ella May tried to smile. "I hear bells. They couldn't be church bells." She moved under the covers. "They must be cowbells."

"Possibly so. Here, raise up your hips a wee trifle. Let me spread this rubber sheet there under you. Here. That is fine. Now. Lift your feet and legs. Do you feel any terrible pains? Here. Now. There. Isn't that better? Is it not?" Blanche's hands put the rubber sheet in place before the drafts of cold wind could reach Ella May's skin. "There are no other kinds of bells that ring out here on these plains that I know of. How is that, now?"

"Better. Yes. But I, ah, see ten million faces inside of bells. Half like bells. Half like people singing. I see the people in the bells and the bells in the people. And they're all a-ringing together. All ringing at the same time. All together." Ella May's lips fell wide apart, she spoke her words against her pillow. The warmth from her breath on the slip felt good against her eyebrow and she moved her cheek closer to the warm spot. "Every cowbell has ten people inside it, and ten people come and go with every cowbell. Ten people live, ten people die, and the cowbell keeps going on. And every time the old cow rings her bell on her neck, ten people talk the dingle of the jingle. And when the old cow is measured and sold the bell goes away with her or the bell falls somewhere behind, and somebody's toe stumbles across it where it fell, and the voices are in it. But the voices have just been lost in the mud and dried in the dirt. And I'm walking and I'm looking. And so this is me here walking and looking. And I never did to my soul know why, but I always did get the best feeling in the world, just, just out of finding an old brassy cowbell. I see it dried in the dirt. I stop and I dig it out. I clean it out good and then I take hold of the handle or the strap and I shake it just as hard as I can. And of course it doesn't ring. It won't ring because I left some plugs of dirt in it. So I feel away up inside of it with my finger and I dig out the crusts of dirt. Rain-mixed, sun-dried dirt. All kinds of horse hoofs wading around in the mud. Men and women with their kids tromping loose hay and grass, dry manure, down in and through the mud. And they push the cowbell down into the mud and they cut it up into big square blocks. And while they lift and haul and work, once in a while the cowbell will ring, just a little dingle, just ever so little a dingle. But all of their voices I hear inside the brass of the bell. And when they cut the square blocks, isn't it funny? Their voices soak into the sun-dried bricks. And when the bricks are lifted up into a house, then all of their yelling, joking, laughing, crying, everything, is all in the walls and the ceilings, and the floors, and the yards and the fields and the house. Crazy. Silly old, goofy old cowbells."

Blanche worked fast about the room. She took a white slipover uniform from her suitcase under the bed and tied her hair up tight in a colored handkerchief. She heard a sound in Ella's talk that could have been caused by a fever from some sort of a pain that Ella tried to hide. A rambling delirious tone. A flow of words from some unconscious place. Ella had not labored long enough to be so feverish. Blanche shook a thermometer and put it under Ella's tongue.

Ella May's face felt a bit too hot to the touch of Blanche's hand, but she guessed this was because her hand was cold from dabbling in the water on the stove. Through the black glass of the north window Blanche saw the first flakes of snow fly in the storm. The wind had blown too hard for the past few hours, the night had been too cold, the clouds had blown too fast, too high, for the snow to form. "A blue blizzard is not a blue blizzard unless the snow blows in with it," she said to herself. But her words must have been louder than she guessed because Ella May covered her pains with a smile and answered with the glass tube in her mouth, "Unless th' shnow jusht blowshhh itshelf to death itsh not a genuine blue blizhard." And Blanche pushed her hand against Ella's forehead saying, "Do not try to talk. You will swallow the thermometer. I haven't got another."

And then through the blow of the snow they both heard again the ring of Tike's shovel against the deeper dirt by the shed.

"There'sh my bellsh. See?" Ella stiffened herself.

"I told you to lay still. Be quiet. I don't hear any bells.

I only hear Tike up in the attic with his tractor parts. Will you please please be quiet just for a while, Ella May? I want to see if you're running any fever. Still."

"That Tike is forever and forever working with those old parts. He thinks that he can build a new tractor out of them. You don't hear any bells?" Ella May rolled on her pillow. She opened her eyes a tiny slit and the whirl of the room before her caused her to shut them again with a squint. "People? Bells?"

"Quit your dreaming." Blanche lifted the thermometer from Ella's lips and held it up in the lamplight. "It is too hard on you. Hmmm."

"I think you are just lying," Ella told Blanche. "You are just an old liar. Liar woman. Liar woman all dressed up to fool me. I'd rather to dream than to live and not be able to." And then a bit later she said, "Dream."

"Hush. I thought so. You're feverish. Two points above. Hmmm." Blanche tapped her fingernails against the iron vines and flowers at the head of the bed. "Anything else hurting you besides your baby? Is there? Any other pains anywhere? I have to know. Is there?"

"No. You lied to me. Hush. I wouldn't tell you if I had a red-hot stove poker stuck in my chest. I've told you ten dozen or more times, no. No. No. Just the baby."

"Any sprains? Bruises? Headaches? Have you hurt yourself in any way that pains you?" Blanche wiped the thermometer on a white cloth, then dropped it into its case and down in her pocket. "You have more pain than you should at this early hour. If you feel any others, tell me. I have to know."

"Just the baby. Drawing. Pushing. This pushing down. All of this. Just the baby. After this is over, I'll be fine and dandy," Ella lied, but her story had a truthful sound.

Blanche knew that if the pains were causing so much delirium and fever at this early hour, she could expect things to get several times worse before the child saw lamplight. She had seen other cases where old forgotten sore spots, bone and ligament bruises, sprains and fractures, had flashed back into the mind of the woman again to hurt her and frighten her to such a degree that her muscles were tight, nerves tense, and the birth was delayed for several hours and became twice as painful and far more dangerous. She could treat such a thing now if only Ella May would point out to her any such places of pain caused by old hurts. There was pressure on one or more of her nerves, there were feverish worries in her brain. These caused all of the earlier pains to magnify and, already, to run into rambles of unconscious speech. Possibly she could trace it down as the night wore on.

Tike dragged his shovel back across the yard and listened to it ring down against the hard-frozen ground. It rang louder when he tossed it up against the side of the house. He was a walking bag of fears and hopes and the ringing was still in his words when he shoved the door open and said, "Snowin' ta beat hell out there. Say, ain't I a papa yet, after all my diggin' and freezin'?"

In the blowing flame of the lamp he saw Blanche with her finger against her lips, and his words trailed off down the Cap Rock. He ducked his head in bashful sorrow because he had let it slip his mind Ella was not to know that he had been digging a hole in the sod to bury her afterbirth in.

"Shh." Blanche could not be seen any too plainly in the flicker of the lamp. But her "Shh" was plainer than any snake that Tike had ever heard hiss in the grass.

"Tikey Doodle?" Ella's voice was high, scattered, broken off into loose stems, then drowned out by a howl of swift wind whining up under the floor. "You? Tikey Dude?"

"No tellin' what you'll think to call me next." He slid out of his coat and sweater and hung them up on their nails. "Yes. This is me. Where's my brat? I mean baby? I come ta git 'im."

"You will catch your death of dampness up there in that old roost. You just leave those old tractor parts go until some day when it is warmer." Her words were strained through the bedclothing.

Tike looked at Blanche with his mouth open. "Ahhh. Roost? Ah. But, Lady," and then he fished for a story. "Ahh, honest ta God, Lady, I got th' best tractor in Texas put together up there. It's a su'prize! Soooprize! We're gonna take on six hundred more acres of wheat land, Lady! Six hundred! I took alla them ole parts, an' took 'em, an' I twisted 'em, I mean, I took 'em, an' I wired 'em all up together! All together! An' I made the biggest pertiest tractor in th' world!"

"I have not entertained the slightest inkling of a doubt."

Ella's laugh dealt her more pain above her breast. "And just what is the name of it? Your tractor?"

"Ahhh. Hamlin. HAMLIN! Better'n any other kind on th' market! Just wait'll ya rub yer eye out on it!"

"I'm simply dying to."

That word *dying* sent trembles of icy sweat up and down Tike's backbone, but he shuffled from one foot to the other and tried to act braver. "You'll hear plenty about it. Don't worry. Just take it easy and let that little Tike Hamlin git outta yer belly first, 'cause I cain't git my tractor down outta th'roost without his help. So just lie there, an' don't worry, an' take yer pace easy. 'Cause he's, he's th' only one can lift it down while I hold the roof up fer 'im." He felt such a shaking in his body that he started to fall to his knees and crawl over to the side of the bed. It was Blanche that motioned him back with her hands as if to say, "We don't want to get her all nervous again."

"Is that your new tractor that I hear running? Or is that a feather floating through the air?"

Blanche motioned him back again. He hated her for waving him about in his own house, and a thousand curse words flew onto his tongue. He kept his lips closed as tight as he could and managed to swallow his words. He would remember it, though, and mow her down with them the very first time he caught her out of Ella's presence.

"That noise that you hear? That?" He put his hand to his ear and walked to the north window. "That's them old loud noisy snowflakes out there running into one another.

And they're a-makin' so much of a damned racket that I cain't even hear my new tractor run. Lissen. Lissen. Nope. Them goldern snowflakes. Cain't hear my tractor engine."

There was a faint frown on Blanche's face as she moved her eyes up and down in an effort to get a look into Ella's eyes. Was this horseplay back and forth between Mr. and Mrs. Hamlin a good or a bad thing for the baby? Well, it had its good parts. Ella had turned quieter, less strained. Tike's eyes were so filled with the wild lamplight that he looked like a fiery-eyed devil to his own self as he saw the things of the room reflected in the whipped snows out the north window glass. And the feeling that came over him as he saw his eyes shine outside was, "I'm a devil. I'm a devil with nine little devils dancin' off my prong." Of course, these were his thoughts, his whole feelings. But his feelings whirled and stirred in with the norther and he went right on being a devil. He blew his hot breath against the cold glass and drew a circle, two dots for eyes, a new moon for a mouth, two new moons for horns, and laughed. "Hey. Blanche. Wanta see th' baby's pitcher? Huh?" And when Blanche took a step or two across the floor and looked at his artwork with a cold disgust, Tike slapped his hands against his knees and stood there laughing for a good long time.

"If I was your wife and I was having a baby and you would make such a picture of it on the window glass, believe me, I would get a broom and wear it out on your head." And Blanche took a short walk around the room to see if all of the needs of the night were in their proper order. She spoke each word as she looked. "Soap. Water. Cloths. Towels. Washrags. Rubber sheets. Gloves. Chloroform. Cotton. Papers. Tools and scissors." And then she lifted her fingers toward her black suitcase and nodded at its contents.

"Hey, Blanche," Tike said when she came near his window. "I betcha that whenever ya see this here baby, you'll want one exactly like it. Jist wait."

"Hot water. Broom. Mop. Oh. Huh? I will bet. I know that I will just simply go wild to have one. Lots of other proud poppies have told me the same story. But so far they are all mistaken. Matches. Alcohol."

"You'll see. Jist watch."

"You are trying to make me a joke. But I really would like to have a baby. I admit." She looked out into the north.

"Make ya a big barg'in."

"What?"

"I'll give ya th' pertiest baby on all these north an' south plains if ya'll come an' help me build my earth house."

"Doesn't your brain function on any other subject except just this business of making babies?" Blanche blew her own breath on the glass and drew circles with dots for eyes, noses, and mouths.

Tike touched his finger to the glass and added half-moon devil's horns to Blanche's faces and said, "Nope. Nuthin' else. Makin' babies. An' earth houses to raise 'em in."

Blanche drew bare trees, sprigs of grass, weeds, all around the edge of the windowpane. In order to keep the upper hand in this situation, she shook her head seriously, slowly, pooched her lips, and said, "I know that you are just fooling me, Tike. I mean, Mister Hamlin. But I really do want a baby. Not just only one baby, but I want several nice boys and several nice girls. And of course I really and truly want a nice big weatherproof house, possibly the earth kind that you keep talking about. And since I must have a man, naturally, before I can have my babies and my house, I will remember you, and I will certainly keep such a great inventor, ahhh, builder of, ahhh, Hamlin tractors in mind. But of course, this country is a free country, and I do feel that you should allow me the full freedom and the full liberty to consider possibly one, maybe two or three, other men for the job. You agree?"

"Shore. Shore. Ya mean ya might? Might take me up?" Tike's face in the glass was serious. "Chance, huh?"

"A chance?" Blanche ridiculed him. "Of course there is a chance. A chance and more than a chance."

Tike's head shook till his neck was tired as he repeated her words. "More'n jist a chance? More'n jist a chance? Huh? Hey. Ha."

"After all, you are a man and I am a woman. And the force that draws the man together with the woman is larger and stronger than the powers that drive little tractors to plow and to reap, or that blow little blue northern blizzards down on top of the people's houses."

Tike's eyes stood open like saucers of milk and his mouth was a cavern filled with bats. "Uh-huh. Yeah. Gosh."

"A man and a woman must get together. They must find

one another somewhere in these storms of life. They must cling and hold and come together. They must. They just just just just must."

"Yep."

"And after all, I am a pretty girl when I get my things taken off. There is nothing seriously wrong with my legs, and my waist will not get much larger. I am rosy of cheek and full of breast. I look at myself in the mirror and I think how bad I really do need a man and all of these little babies that you keep talking about. And after all, for you, young, thirty-three, strong, fairly slim, not any too wise, but fiery and windburned. For you, don't you think that there is more than just a chance?"

Tike had shaken his head so long and so fast that he could not control it, nor stop it. He tried to say something, but only managed to stammer, stutter out some loose words.

"There are not more than, well, say, fifteen or sixteen million people out in these midwestern states, and I do not guess that more than six or seven million of them are men. The rest of them are women, and naturally I would not marry any of the women, so it is only the men that I could possibly marry, and here you are, right here, and I know a good bit about you. I am familiar with some of your little ways and I understand you very well. It is just these other six, seven million that I will have to look over and pick from. So the wind is blowing your way, after all. You see? Now when you foolishly asked me a minute ago if there was a chance for you and I to have babies together, earth houses together, you did not see how close you were to hitting the head on the nail, did you?"

"Huh-uh." Tike was feeling his legs with his hands down in his pockets. He leaned back against the wall, half drifting out into the piling, blowing snow. "Gosh no. I, ahh, er, didn't see that I was hittin' my, ahh, head on no, ahhh, nail." And then he thought of how silly the whole conversation had sounded, and he dropped his gaze down along the bottom of the window and saw the snow blow in and mix with the dust.

Ella May grunted and laughed to herself on her bed. Blanche left Tike leaning against his window frame and walked across the floor to Ella's side. "Did you hear your husband and I talking?" Blanche asked. And Ella May laughed again and said, "No, I just got tickled at the way this little army is fighting for its freedom here in my stomach. Fighting to see the light of day. Or the dust."

Tike talked to his own self. He moved his fingers in front of him like a mud-digging machine and said, "Hmmmphh. Hell, I could build ten houses outta earth 'fore I could ever git ta first base with a godblame gal like Blanche is."

HAMMER RING

The dark had set in early, around six o'clock, and Ella May's pains had started at almost straight up nine thirty. Blanche kept the water boiling, and everything that she would need was almost at her fingertips. She had changed Ella from her housedress into a clean white cotton night-gown, and the snow outside had managed to catch a foot-hold and to lie on the ground. The wind carried looser snow in whirls and clouds, and the speed of the wind seemed to be faster, louder, lonesomer. And the hours of her first pains had gone past for Ella May as slow and as gay, as dreary, as mixed up, as the snows outside. And now the alarm clock on its orange-crate shelf said that it was half past one on the new morning. Ella's real birth pains had come over her, and it caused Tike to walk the floor, to rub his hands together, to pull at his nails, rub his cheeks, his neck, and he had pulled at his ears till a soreness shot through both sides of his head.

In his high nervous temper he said in his mind, "That Blanche is just coldhearted, that's what she is. She just ain't got no heart about 'er. That's why she can mope along and not get all excited about it. She's got a heart like a marble slab." But further down in him, he knew that he was making up a lie. He knew that he was only defending his own ignorance. What if he was there alone to help Ella bring this little Tike out into this old world? When the thought hit him, he felt as cold and as stiff as a hitch post frozen in the blizzard. He could think of no way to tell how glad he was that Blanche was there, walking around, talking around, doing things easy, doing things right. His head was in such a storm that he had to sit down on the bottom step and hold it in his hands. He brushed his hair with his fingers, patted out tunes with his feet, and he felt his life rise and fall with Ella May's moans and sighs.

Tired of pacing the floor, tired of sitting with his jaws in his hands, tired of trembling like ice on a stem, he stood up and started across the floor to the bed where Blanche watched the pains swell over Ella May. He had taken somewhat less than one step in their direction when Blanche motioned him back with her hand. Just one slight wave of her hand, and not a good healthy wave at that, stopped him dead in his tracks like a buffalo hit between the horns. Just that one little movement of her hand set him burning at the hair roots, fingertips, and toenails. This was the thing that dealt him more misery in one flicker of one short second than all of the other ups and downs of his entire thirty-three years on these plains.

They call you a trained nurse. Well, you listen to me, Misses Trained Nurse. Listen. You just keep quiet and listen

to me. This house ain't mine, because I didn't build it. And
even if it was mine, I wouldn't own it. I wouldn't have the
damned thing if it was wrapped up in Vaseline. But I'm a-
renting it. Renting it, see? Do you savvy that? And I'm the
boss around here till I get to be the boss of some kind of an
earth house or something better. And now if you just happen to be going through the process of forming the opinion
in that brain of yours that you can just sit over there and
wave your hand, or just a finger or two, at me and make me
do dog tricks all over the floor here, well, you're just sadly
mistaken.

But no. Hey. Wait a minute. Don't run off. I guess I flew
off the handle just a shade too quick. After all, I reckon you
did go through with a good bit of trouble to get them trained
nurse papers. It ain't like I was letting you be the boss every
night of the year. I wouldn't let no living woman boss me
around every night in the year. But since it's just this one
night, and you're a visitor in one sense of the word, well,
mebbe, mebbe, I'll let you boss me a little.

Mebbe so. Just a little. After all, when you got company
you got to let them have the run of the place for a little while.
Else they not company. That's all company is. Folks that
come a-running in and take charge of the whole shooting
match. So go on. Wave your finger at me. I got my own
ideas of what to do to make my wife feel like having a baby,
and I'd like to be right over there by the side of her bed. But,
no. No. No. You say I'm full of germs and microbes and
varmints and childs that crawl on the earth. Goshamight

dern whizzers. I'm bigger'n a dang little old germ, ain't I? Ain't I? Look at me? D'ja ever see a deezeeze germ as big as I am? No siree boss you never did, and what's more you never will. I can lick any germ that walks, flies, runs, or crawls. I ain't got no more of them germs on me than you got on you, but I don't wave my finger at you every time you start to take a step toward her bed, do I?

Wouldn't never no babies get born if everybody kep a-waving their fingers and keeping all of the parents back away from the side of the bed. Damn my old hard times to samnation anyhow. Wave your hand. I see it. Wave it. Wave it again. Ain't no earthly feeling on earth feels half as bad as somebody to boss you around with a little old wave of their finger in your own house. It's my wife, ain't it? It ain't your wife. You're a trained nurse. You never will have a wife as long as you live and breathe.

Oh God. God of Jerusalem and Horners Corners. God of all the wigglers and jigglers. Ain't no man a-living can move an inch when a trained nurse in a white uniform shakes her finger at you. It just knocks your props out from under you. Freezes you dead. What in the name of little stepants am I going to do with myself anyhow? Stand up here and walk this floor till I go screwball?

The babies of the upper north plains are born in the pains of the people waiting.

Tike was glad when Blanche nodded her head yes and motioned for him to come closer. He nearly tore the room down getting across the floor. And he heard Ella grit her teeth together as loud as a tractor running over broken bottles, heard her groan in a way that shook him from stem to stern. And yet, along with all of his being afraid, he was wishing in a deeper flow of pride to be in on the deal.

Blanche had to show him what to do with himself. She laughed and thought that he was the one that needed the bed and the treatment and not Ella May.

He saw Ella May's body turn hard, stiff, blue and purple, then pale, then for a moment loose and limber again, then tight. Tight and as hardened as the iron in the sledgehammer, as hard and as tight as strings on a fiddle. She moved her toes and feet as if she were swimming on her back in rough water and there was all over her this same appearance, like she was floating in waters so high that she was almost sucked under every second. Arms and hands fought to keep her balanced, and Blanche showed Tike how to assist in keeping her flat on her back with her legs wide apart.

"Get the broom over there," Blanche nodded, "and let her hold on to the handle. Occupy her hands."

Tike reached into the corner by the radio and put the broom handle into Ella's hands. He saw Blanche splash a few drops of chloroform on some cotton in a paper funnel, and his nose snorted at the burn of the smell. All he could say was, "Like this?"

"Get back of her head there and pull against her. Give her plenty to pull against." Blanche observed the whole thing in much the same manner as a bomber pilot would watch a city below blasted out of its shackles. "Pull. Harder."

"Gosh ding a mighty. Boy. She's got th' power. Damn near jerkin' me through this ironworks here."

"They get as strong as a tractor, all right." Blanche held the funnel of cotton under Ella May's nose for a second or so, then dropped it over onto the eating table. Blanche was well aware of the teasing conflicts that had come between Tike and herself. It was at this moment that she turned into another person entirely. A lady of grace, dignity, seriousness, in absolute command of every move of her entire body. A woman of college in a larger school. All of her fine, precise exactness, her nimble feet, hands, and arms performed with a silent certainty that struck into Tike like lightning in a grove of trees. Her face was not smiling, it was not sad, it was not troubled, and it was not celebrating. It was just her way of moving, her easy come and go. "Strong as a tractor," she said again.

"Nothin' won't go wrong with 'er? Will it?" Tike asked. He watched close. He wondered and he worried and felt some new and very odd thoughts take shape in the room.

He saw the whole baby born. The head first, and he fell to pieces with fear because he thought the pressure of Ella May's muscles would smash it like a cantaloupe.

He saw the head so slick and red, so much soft, all filled with blue and purple blood veins. And he saw every inch of Ella May's body squirm and sway in sobs and moans of pains mixed up with laughs that she laughed just to give him ease. And he saw that for every inch that baby moved Ella May moved in a mile of misery, but a misery that had a smile, a dry joke, a little laugh, even under the chloroform. He felt like Blanche should hold the paper funnel under his own nose and let him sniffle a sniff or two to brace him up. But no. He did not have any bracer of any kind. He was taking the full force of the whole thing head-on, like meeting a truck on the 66. He had saved almost a half pint in a bottle under the house, but it had been knocked down by the hogs and lapped up by the dogs.

Every minute that he worked he shed a gallon of sweat, in spite of such a blowing blizzard one inch through the wall. He held his broom and pulled backward to give Ella's hands and arms something solid to grip on to. His shoes against the floor dragged with a heavy noise, and his trail, if it could be untangled and laid straight, would reach from there to Amarillo. It crossed his mind several times that Blanche was an angel that had grown too wise for the walls of heaven and had flown down in some big wind to warm every house on these high flats. He was inwardly proud of his own work and smiled many times toward Blanche to tell her, "I'm doing my part." The facts were that Blanche smiled even more proud of her own self, as if to say, "I could very easily have tied that broom handle up onto the head of the bed, and allowed you to walk the floor and go out of your mind. I put the broom into your hand to give you something to do, and my, my, just look, you've wrestled with it for over an hour now. And it has kept you from under my feet!"

Tike could see the hooded veil of wet skin over the head, and he thought of the thousands of times he had heard his folks say, "This person will be gifted with powers and knowledge because he was born with a veil over his face." Or say, "This lady knows the things of the past, present, and the future, and knows what is on your mind because she had a veiled birth." And hundreds of other things he had heard them say. How much he believed these things he did not know at this moment, but when his eyes saw the veil as clear as day all over the head and the face there, he felt the pride of the plains drift through him like a wind.

He saw the shoulders come out into sight, and then the stomach moved faster, the hips a bit slower, and then Blanche held her hands flat under the back and lifted the legs outward somewhat easier. The faster the thing moved, the better Tike felt. He lived several years of his life with every inch of the baby that slid out into Blanche's hands. And she seemed to be as much at home and at ease as Grandma Hamlin would have been right there in the room. "Will she drop it? Don't let it slip. Hold on. Don't break it. Hey, you're letting its head fall back too far there. Watch out for the feet there, they're all covered up with a lot of other junk and things. What is all of that stuff?" He felt Ella May's hands turn loose from the handle of the broom and saw them fall down on the pillow by her head. He stood the broom up in the corner and took a few steps around Blanche's back to the side of the bed. His eyes tried to take in the whole thing all at one big sweep, and then he shook his head till he caught control of his breath and asked Blanche, "*SSSsssttt*. What's alla that there extra stuff there? God. Somethin's bad wrong."

He nodded his head at the baby as Blanche laid its head on Ella's thigh, cleaned its face, and rubbed Ella May's stomach with her left hand. Tike felt the sun and the moons of a hundred sunstrokes sail through his eyes when he caught sight of three or four large pieces of meaty organs, ropes of intestinal tubes, burst bags of water, and he felt even weaker as he saw more and more tissues work their way out from the outer lips of Ella May's womb. A greasy water was all over Blanche's hands and arm, the baby, Ella May's thighs and hips, and puddles as deep as a domino were standing about the baby's rump on the sheet. He breathed so loud and swallowed so hard that Blanche heard him. She knew the nature of his worry, and for a joke she told him, "Maybe it would be good if you would smell of the chloroform."

"Yeah." Tike took the joke to be serious. He held the paper of cotton under his nose and took a deep breath. "Whewww! God. Whatta lick! Ahhh. Anything go wrong? What's all that other stuff there? Everything okay, Blanche?" He pointed to the bed.

Blanche watched his finger shake and told him, "Yes. That is the afterbirth. Everything is all right. There will be some more come along in a bit. You put that chloroform down. It will make you float out through the ceiling."

"I wish't I could," Tike said in back of her.

"You should not feel that way. Don't be so depressed. Look. You are the proud father of a nice big healthy hale and hearty baby boy! See!" She fetched the baby up again between her hands and took away all of the excess organs and tissues. With both hands she held the baby up as high as the umbilical cord would allow. Then she blew her breath into the face and patted the little purplish red rump with the palm of her right hand. Tike took a step closer to take it from her arms because he had never seen any child spanked in any such a way as this. As he moved near her, Blanche shoved him back away with her left elbow and blew her breath again. "Commy commy come on. Commy commy come on. Wakey wakey wake up. Wakey wakey wake up you. Here. *Tsssttt*. Timey timey for you to wake uppy. Blooooo!" And Tike heard her spank harder and louder against the wrinkled, scrawny-looking skin of the rump. "Bloooo. Blooo. Blooo!" Blanche made quick moves with the baby in the air above Ella May's stomach.

And something more than the heat and the cold and the hail and the rains of the gumbo plains shook in Tike Hamlin's soul as he stood there, insulted, hurt, afraid, nervous, proud, glad, miserable.

A noise came. A noise in the whole room. A noise from under the bed, in the closet, up the stairs, even down from the roost, from out the cans of cream, the disks of the separator, the tablecloth, out of the globe of the lamp, the sound came onto the air, through the sounds of the night winds outside, the creaking of snow and ice, the scrunch of crusted sleets, hard froze snow, a cry. It was a scattered and a broken, windblown, rattling yell. It was a woman drowned in water, a man drowned in hot oil. A dog that fell from a land-

slide down the Cap Rock. A mama turkey shrieking at three
of her babies caught in the mud ruts under truck wheels.
The last death hiss, the only live sound of the leather lizard
under a fallen rock. Noise of dry locusts on stems of bushes.
High rattle of clouds of grasshoppers peeling off across the
ranch. A yelping dog. Hungry coyote. The croak of a carp
feeding with his fins out of water, the gasp of the buzzard
shot through the head. A sound of new green things crash-
ing up out of the spring ground. A dry wagon wheel, a barn
door, the jingle of rusty spurs hung on the windmill post.
The sound was a cry and the cry had all of these sounds and
more and other sounds, all of the sounds, all of the hisses,
barks, yelps, whoops, croaks, peeps, chirps, screams, whis-
tles, moans, yells, and groans, all of these were mixed up in
Tike's head as he listened to the screak of the bones of his
temples and saw Blanche shake his baby there above that
slick wall canyon. And out of the walls of the canyon the cry
got itself together, and it got better organized and unionized
and turned into something so wide, so high, so big, so loud,
that it strained the boards of the shack. When it did dawn
on Tike that all of this sounding was coming out from the
mouth and the lungs, the belly, of his baby there in the air
over that bed, then a feeling of such pride came over him
that he felt like a blacksmith's anvil, and he heard in his soul
a hundred hammers ring. And he heard his own hammer
ring on every other anvil in the whole world. Proud. That
is only a word, a sound made by the tricks of the tongue,

lips, teeth. And when Tike heard the baby twist its face into knots and scream out over Ella May, he felt like one of the folks that live happy on the earth.

The baby twisted its face into every shape, and Ella May smiled out through the fogs and mists of the chloroform. Blanche pinched the cord between her thumb and finger about halfway between Ella May's stomach and the baby's navel. She put the baby down on its back to scratch and to howl out against the opinions of the entire world. Tike did not feel like he was smiling inside himself, because what Blanche had done seemed to shovel a bucket of red-hot coals into the furnace of his brain. She worked swift as the running rabbit, and with both hands down against the sheet. The digested food inside the cord she pushed back toward Ella's stomach and an inch or so in the baby's direction, then held a finger tight under the cord, snipped it in two with one whack of her scissors. The ends that had been squeezed empty of foodstuffs she tied into knots exactly like the knot on a catgut fiddle string. Ella May's end of the cord moved back into the lips of her womb. Tike saw Blanche tie one more such knot close up to the baby's belly, then snip off a few of the extra inches with the scissors. She left a few inches hanging down from the navel. The empty cord bled a few drops of watery liquid around the rims, but to Tike the whole sight was a bloody wreck on a fast road.

"What's th' loose end a-hangin' down like that for? Hey. Look. Blanche. Didn't ya mess somethin' up? Gosh damn a mighty. Kill a man in agony to stan' here an' watch sucha sight. Hey. Do somethin'. Fix it. That loose bloody end there. Look."

"Stand back. Don't breathe so close to the bed. That loose end will dry up and disappear in a few days and you won't even be able to see it. Stand back. Don't hold your hand over that bed. Germs."

"Germs. God damn germs. 'At's all I heard outta you since you been here. Germs. Ain't no germ gonna keep me from a-takin' up for my own kid. Germs. Germs." He backed away. "Hey. Ella. Lady. Hey. How d'ya feel? Lady?"

And through the lashes of her closed eyes Ella May looked still a few degrees dizzy on the chloroform. "Is it. A boy. Or. A girl?"

"A real nice big boy." Blanche lifted the baby down between its mother's feet and rubbed oil onto its skin. "A big bounder, too."

"Hold still, there, Grasshopper!" Tike spoke out. He stood a few feet, one or two, from the side of the bed and leaned over as far as Blanche would allow.

Ella's lips were hot, damp with a juice that covered her whole body with a look of healthy pinkness. "Boy? Who said a grasshopper?"

Blanche kept quiet and worked with the oil. Her caresses and rubs on his wary limbs made him coo and smile with vast satisfaction.

"I just called 'm a little grasshopper. He's a boy. Lady. Justa 'bout th' finest feller I've laid my two eyes on. Lissen to 'im coo. Watch that little ornery rapscallion smile when

Blanche, when a perty gal, rubs his stummick. Ya. Ha. Boy! Yepsir. He's a boy, all right, and he's all boy, too. Gosh, ya'd outghta get a look at 'im, Lady." Tike had invented purely by accident some sort of a dance, a dance much like the one the early tribes now buried in the shale of the Cap Rock danced, possibly the world's simplest and one of its most graceful dances. A dance that is danced standing still. Tike's two feet were still, yet the rest of him danced on the floor and the door and at the mouths of rivers. The room danced together with him, and as he watched Ella May breathe and move slightly there on her bed, he saw that her face, her eyes, her thoughts, danced out past the shack. Tike had to stand still. He did not want to move any farther backward, and Blanche would not let him carry his germs any closer to the bed, so he swayed, moved, in every possible way that he could as he stood in his tracks.

"But. It couldn't be a grasshopper," Ella May nearly whispered. "It just couldn't be."

"Quit your worrying." Blanche wrapped a white flannel blanket around the baby and laid him out on top of the covers. "Help me here to get this rubber sheet out from under her."

The two of them removed the rubber sheet from beneath Ella May's hips, back, shoulders, legs, and feet, little by little, inch by inch. Lifting, bracing, holding Ella May so that the weight did not fall on the weak muscles of her body.

And as soon as the rubber sheet was rolled into a bundle, Blanche carried it to the door. Tike stole another step closer

while her back was turned and waved his hands in a dozen
foolish fashions at the child and at Ella May. He made the
new noises that had sounded in his ears at the baby's first
cry. "Oggle ma google dee boogle ma stoofge. Iggle dee
wiggle ma jiggle dum bittle. Unky de dunk. Unku de dunk.
Blamm. Whammm. Singo blingo blango. Clunkity clink.
Blinkety blink. Ha. Hey! Look! I'm a father! Heeeyy! You
damn old blizzard out there a twistin' yer tail off, look! Yay-
hooo!" He pounded his fists against his chest until his un-
dershirt was nearly in shreds, howling, "Yayhoo! I'm a god
dern papa! Daddy! Fatherrr! Hey, Lady, I'm a fatherrr!"

Ella May only smiled back at him, then down at her boy
in his blanket. She smiled alike at her two boys. The look on
her face was the same for Tike as for the grasshopper. She
felt freer, easier, lighter since the eighteen or so pounds of
baby and his trimmings were now outside her stomach. The
chloroform still cast banks of wild snow and summer whirlwinds across her mind. She felt a bit like Tike was taking
just a pinch too much credit for the birth, but she felt so glad
for him that she allowed him to steal the whole show. His
actions refreshed her, caused her to take deeper breaths, to
begin to move her feet and legs and to feel the good heat of
her skin against the gray cotton blankets. The rubber sheet
had been cold. Tike tried to play with the baby and to cover
Ella May up at the same time, but Blanche put her hand on
his shoulder and said, "Take your germs and stand back."

"I guarantee you one thing right here and now," Tike
told the other three. "Just as quick as this cold weather

breaks, me an' this little grasshopper here is gonna plow up some rooty sod an' cut us out some big thick bricks an' build us a house of earth. An' it's gonna have walls so thick that they cain't no wind git in, an' cain't no varmints crawl in, an' cain't no weather of no kind git in, an they damn sure cain't no dern'd ole germs be a-bustin' in an' a-gittin' onto me an' a-keepin' me separated fr'm my wife an' my little grasshopper there. This is me tellin' yoooo, all of yooo!" And he waved his fists through the room.

Ella May's stomach moved up and down when she laughed.

Blanche thought that Tike was causing just a wee bit too much of an uproar in the room for this particular stage of the show, and she tossed her look about the room for some kind of a job for him. It had to be a job that would take him up into the roost and occupy his mind for the next several minutes, at least, to give her time to put the baby on the pillow at Ella May's side. Wait. What was it? Oh . . . Yes. "Tike."

"It'll have walls, by God, and little hookworms, as thick as that there warsh bench over there. Mebbe thicker. My house is gonna be so thick that nothin' could ever run it down. An' no goddamn little ole measly germ's gonna even find him a sneak hole ta git in at!"

"Tike. Will you please quit pacing up and down the floor, please? You are shaking the bed too much."

"My house won't shake. Won't shake no bed this time next year. You just come back out here an' stick yer head in on us an' you'll see. You can jump up an' down, hit th' walls, bounce up against th' ceilin', do any damn thing ya wanta do, an' that there house'll just reach down and grab a hold of th' ole earth, an' say, Hell, you cain't shake no floor o' mine, no matter how hard ya pace up an' down it. See? I mean it. I'll buy that acre of Cap Rock land off from ole man Woodridge an' pay 'im his price fer it. I'll git th' money. I can git th' money. Don't you worry. Just don't you worry." And he paced the floor so heavy that the house shook the bed even more.

"Go take your shovel and bury that afterbirth. I will give you a job pacing the yard outside, if you must pace." Blanche worked about the bed. She fixed this, straightened that. Put this in place. "Hurry. It will stink up the house."

"You don't believe that, do you? I mean about my house made out of earth? Huh? You don't think an ole down-an'-out sharecropper like me c'n make the riffle from an ole crappy shack like this into a nice dirt house with big thick walls, do ya?"

"I don't know, Tike." Blanche felt like he was directing his words at the wrong person somehow. Yet she had gotten used to this business where her patients carried all of their troubles and hopes to her just because she had educated her hands to take a baby from the stomach of a woman. "Why should I know? I don't believe that anybody with any real nerve 'bout them, any real brains, would let themselves fall down so low as to live another minute in an old filthy mousetrap like this. But as to your dream house, your, what you call your house of earth, well, where it is going to come up from, I do not know. I don't seem to be able to see right at this moment. Now if you will wait a minute while I put the baby right there at its mother's side and there, cover it up good, there like that, now, when you go out the door, open it and shut it very quickly, very quick, so as not to set up too much of a draft through the house. Hurry. And bundle yourself up really warm and good. And, Tike. Be sure to tell me how cold it is outside when you get back. There is the sheet, there by the door. Carry it with the ends tucked in good so as not to spill its contents in the yard. Easy with the door." She bent over the baby and Ella May to shelter them from the cold draft of air that shot through the house for a second as Tike walked out.

"How do you like him?" Blanche lifted the boy up before Ella's eyes.

"He already looks tough as leather, doesn't he?" Ella May's talk already had that deeper sound. "Except that his skin is all wrinkled up. Is there anything the matter with him? Look there around his knees and his neck and everywhere. He looks more like a Cap Rock lizard, with his skin all dried up and wrinkled, than like a son of mine."

Blanche's hands held him. Her eyes roamed up and down all over him. He kicked, he elbowed things out of his way, he made secret signals to the ships lost in the summer mirages. He clenched his two fists and thrashed them in the air. "It seems like all of us are born to look like canyon lizards, monsters, snakes, or fishes of some kind, baby elephants, or something. But it's going to be your job, Mrs.

Hamlin, to see that he grows up out of all of this, and grows into a man."

"You know, Blanche, there while I was under that ether or chloroform . . ."

"Chloroform."

"Whatever it was. I had the craziest dreams. Visions."

And both of them could hear through the outside wind the ring of Tike's long-handled shovel against the earth, frozen hard as granite.

"Yes?"

"I saw this little old crazy rotten room just whirl, and whirl, and then it blew up. Blew up. Like a big firecracker. And then I saw Tike. He was running his self crazy trying to chase down all of the blown-up pieces and bring them all back together again. And I said to him, 'Tike, you are the craziest man living, it's already blown up and knocked sky high and crooked and it's in a million billion pieces. Let it go. You're just crazy to try to chase all over the plains for nothin'. But we don't have any other house to go into,'" Ella May said as she continued to talk about her vision in a disjointed way. "And so, I guess that this junk pile is still just one inch better than having the baby outside in the ice of the blizzard. Listen. Listen. Hear that? That is Tike's hammer, I mean, Tike's shovel ringing on the ground. That will give you a very good idea of how hard that soil is frozen. Hear?"

And in the four walls of the room the breath of Blanche, the heavier breathing of Ella May, the whipping, flying sounds of the storm, mixed, stirred, and blended with the ringing of the shovel, the flicker of the lamp, the noises from the mouth of the grasshopper.

"Just how any such a flimsy rickety trap as this can stand up in the weight of such a wind and snow is a mystery, a mystery I never will be able to figure out. The good Lord must be holding it up there on the south side with His right shoulder."

"I don't know about the Lord." Blanche sat as easily as she could on the edge of the bed near Ella's feet. She smiled because the cry of the boy already sounded clearer, healthier, his mouth and throat had spat out some of the phlegm, spit, slobber, saliva, that had caused him to rattle and to hiss. Blanche was proud of her job. She always felt as great a weight lifted from her as was removed from the stomach of each mother. She rubbed her fingers lightly on the fuzz of the top blanket and kept her eyes on the shape of the boy. "I think that the Lord, or Jesus, would have already knocked this shack down with one slap of His hand. And He would already have told Mister Woodridge to let you build your house of earth here on this spot. If the Lord had His way about it your baby would not have to be born in this hole of sickness and death, but in your new warm healthy house built out of earth."

"But what would Woodridge say if Jesus was to reach down out this blizzard and slap this shack down?"

"I guess that Woodridge would call the deputies and the police and the city hall and Coxley's Army and all of the alligators and yellow dogs and have them track Jesus down through the ice and the snow and lock Him up for a year or two. And if Jesus tried to help you build this other house you talk about, I don't know, but I think that they would lock Him up for fifty years, ninety-nine years."

"Surely they wouldn't. Why, this hull isn't worth two drops of my baby's spit. And a house made out of earth bricks like we intend to build, really the actual money it would take to put it up would be even less than the amount that it took to build this one-room outfit. Do you think anybody would get mad at the Lord if he was to help us put up our new place? Who? Why, the money isn't really enough for anyone to get mad about. It's not that."

"It is that." Blanche touched the tip of her finger to cover over the baby's knee. "It is just that."

"Just what?"

"Just what you said. Because the earth house is so strong that it will stand for two hundred years. Because it has walls eighteen inches thick. Because it is warm in the winter, cool in the summer. Because it is easy to build and does not require any great skill to build it. Because it does not eat nickels and drink dollars, and because it needs no paint, because you do not have to work your heart and soul away and carry every penny into town to lay on the top of Mister Woodridge's desk. Because of this. Because of all of these things. Because your house could be six rooms instead of this eighteen feet of disease. Because you could pay out the earth house in a year or two and it would belong to you. Because it would not belong to them. After all these years they are still bleeding the people for rent, payments, this kind, that kind, on these rusted-out, rotted-down, firetrap wood skeletons. If Jesus was to help you to get free from their trap, they would lay Him away behind bars."

"I just can't, cannot, to save my soul, bring myself to believe that any earthly human could possibly do such a mean trick. I think that old Woodridge does what he does because the Lord tells him what is best for him. Maybe the Lord told him that it is right and good to keep all of this land in one big block and not to build any houses on it. It would be easier to work in one big block. He could make better use of his tractors, save fuel, save on seed bills, and, after all, the house of the families that work on the land can just as easy be built over there on that Cap Rock cliff where the wheat don't grow. This is wonderful wheat land right here under this old shack, and I think Woodridge is absolutely right in saying that he wants to tear it away and till this land. This one little acre here will feed many a hungry mouth every year." All during the talk, Ella moved the baby closer against her side, and with her arm she squeezed him lightly with each word. "In fact, I was just intending to ask you to take my two hundred dollars to Woodridge's office in the next day or two and buy that acre over there on the Cap Rock."

"You know that I will be glad to do it." Blanche spoke softly and quiet. All of this conversation was not too beneficial to Ella's nerves right at this point. "Woodridge is possibly doing what he thinks is best. And to buy the Cap Rock acre for two hundred dollars is not wrong—no, I did not say that it was. But this is just where your troubles will start. It will be a hard fight. A fight with the lumberyard, a fight with the loan company, because you will find out that no bank will even lend as much as one dollar with which to build your earth house."

"I'm not afraid of the hard part." The noises of the boy made her eyes smile. Ella's face plowed itself into long furrows as she thought deeper. "But Blanche, we have mortally got to get our little grasshopper out of this old crate. And into our other house. And I know how to fight, if it comes to that.

"I sometimes wonder," Ella continued. Blanche wanted to cut the talking as short as she could. Ella needed rest, not speeches. Blanche got up and busied herself with the buckets and pots of water on the stove. "I wonder if it will ever come to an out-and-out fight. I sometimes hope so. I wish that the families of people that live in debt all of their lives in their trash-can houses would all get together and fight to get out of the miserable stink and mess. I wish they could know as I know that they work and pay out their good money just for the privilege of living in a coffin.

"A coffin?" Ella moved in bed. "A good coffin would cost more than a dozen of these shacks. A graveyard spot would cost more. Oh, it is just so expensive to die these days. This is the reason why I want to keep on staying alive. And I want to show just a few people around here that there is a way to come out of this mess, to build a better house, and not pick up and run away down the highway. I'll be one that'll never take to that road that goes nowhere. I can stand out there in this yard on a clear day and see the spot where I was born, see the old spot where Tike was born, I can see the old spots where all of our folks were born. And I just feel like I would go out of my mind entirely if I had to wake up every morning somewhere, away off in a place where I would get up and look out and not see all of these old spots. I don't know what shape it will take, work or fight, or burn or freeze or what, but I do know this one thing. I am put here to stay."

To quiet her a bit, Blanche said, "Shh. What is that?"

Ella was still. "Tike singing. He always gets to singing when he hears iron or steel ringing."

"Listen."

Little Grasshopper when he was a baby
Well, he hopped up on his mommy's knee
And he grabbed up a tractor in his right hand
Says, "Tractor be th' death of me! Oh, God!
Tractor be th' death of me!"

"Listen to him make that shovel ring right in with his singing. If you would call that singing," Ella said. "But the only thing is, it sounds more like he was dying or something."

Blanche smiled over her work at the stove and listened.

The landlord he told the little Grasshopper
I'm gonna drive my tractor plow out on this farm
An' I'm a gonna drill that wheat on down, down, down.
I'm a gonna drill that wheat on down!

Tike's song seeped in through the cracks of the boards and in under the wallpaper with a frozen brittle tone. His shovel struck against the icy dirt, and Blanche noticed that he sang in pretty accurate pitch with the ringing.

Well the Grasshopper says to that landlord
You can drive your tractor all around
You can plow, you can plant, you can take in your crop,
But you cain't run my earth house down, down, down!
No! You cain't run my earth house down!

ACKNOWLEDGMENTS

Bringing *House of Earth* alive has been a strange and wonderful experience. Because Woody Guthrie has such a distinctive writing style, it sometimes seemed as though we were communing with the ghost of the typewriter-banging Okie himself. His spirit is very much alive in these pages. Those who decide to enter Woodyland, as we did, never come out the same. There is an old house in the desert near the Chisos Mountains where Guthrie once holed up with his father, brother, and Uncle Jeff. If you visit the ruins, you can almost channel this novel in full.

Sometime in 1947, Guthrie sat down at his typewriter and found the right groove in which to compose *House of Earth*. We've done our best to edit the novel as we believe Woody would have wanted it done. We made a few cosmetic changes and spelling corrections, and some minor restruc-

eddgmentsednodACKNOWLEDGMENTS

turing of two paragraphs. We thought about annotating the novel, but decided it was better to let Woody's prose sing bravely without academic pretense.

Our partner in publishing *House of Earth* is the nonprofit Woody Guthrie Foundation, based in Mount Kisco, New York. All our proceeds from this book will go to the foundation. Never in our experience have we encountered an estate that functions with such loving professionalism. Nora Guthrie, a daughter, is director of the foundation and has spent a lifetime preserving and celebrating all things related to her father. She is a joy to work with. Her family must be smiling down on her from the great beyond.

Through Nora we got to know Tiffany Colannino (archivist) and Barry Ollman (Denver art collector). Both were tremendous to work with.

Two great Guthrie scholars proofread our introduction and Guthrie's novel: Guy Logsdon of Tulsa, Oklahoma; and Professor Will Kaufman of the University of Central Lancashire, author of *Woody Guthrie, American Radical*. We thank Heather Johnson, director of the Northport (NY) Historical Society, who helped us better understand Guthrie's relationship with the Roosevelt administration. Robert Santelli, impresario of the Grammy Museum, shared his hard-earned knowledge of Guthrie with us around every bend. We also benefited mightily from Guthrie's two great biographers: Ed Cray and Joe Klein. Bob Dylan and Jeff Rosen offered us smart feedback after their initial read of the manuscript.

ACKNOWLEDGMENTS

On the production front, special thanks to Virginia Northington of Austin, Texas, for diligently helping to prepare the manuscript for publication. At HarperCollins, we worked with Jonathan Burnham and Michael Signorelli. They were terrific. From the Infinitum Nihil world, special thanks to Christi Depp, Stephen Deuters, Joel Mandel, and Mike Rudell. The audiobook was recorded at both Tequila Mockingbird in Austin and Infinitum Nihil in Los Angeles (thanks, Shayna Brown).

When this novel was first discovered, we collaborated with Pamela Paul and Sam Tanenhaus of the *New York Times Book Review*. They edited our jointly written announcement about *House of Earth*, titled "This Land Was His Land," to coincide almost exactly with the troubadour's one hundredth birthday. We couldn't have found a better outfit to collaborate with.

Douglas Brinkley and Johnny Depp
Albuquerque, New Mexico

SELECTED BIBLIOGRAPHY

Brower, Steven, and Nora Guthrie. *Woody Guthrie Artworks*. New York: Rizzoli, 2005.

Butler, Martin. V*oices of the Down and Out: The Dust Bowl Migration and the Great Depression in the Songs of Woody Guthrie*. Heidelberg: Universitätsverlag, Winter 2007.

Cohen, Ronald. *Woody Guthrie: Writing America's Songs*. New York: Routledge, 2012.

Cray, Ed. *Ramblin' Man: The Life and Times of Woody Guthrie*. New York: W. W. Norton, 2004.

Edgmon, Mary Jo Guthrie, and Guy Logsdon. *Woody's Road: Woody Guthrie's Letters Home, Drawings, Photos and Other Unburied Treasures*. Boulder: Paradigm Publishers, 2012.

Garman, Bryan K. *A Race of Singers: Whitman's Working Class Hero from Guthrie to Springsteen*. Chapel Hill: University of North Carolina Press, 2000.

SELECTED BIBLIOGRAPHY

Guthrie, Nora. *My Name Is New York: Ramblin' Around Woody Guthrie's Town*. Brooklyn: powerHouse Books, 2012.

Guthrie, Woody. *American Folksong*, ed. Moses Asch. New York: Disc Company of America, 1947.

———. *Born to Win*, ed. Robert Shelton. New York: Macmillan, 1965.

———. *Bound for Glory*. New York: E. P. Dutton, 1943.

———. *Every 100 Years: The Woody Guthrie Songbook*, ed. Judy Bell, Anna Canoni, and Nora Guthrie. New York: Hal Leonard, 2012.

———. *Pastures of Plenty*, ed. Dave Marsh and Harold Leventhal. New York: HarperPerennial, 1990.

———. *Seeds of Man: An Experience Lived and Dreamed*. New York: E. P. Dutton, 1976.

———. *Woody Guthrie Folk Songs*, ed. Pete Seeger. New York: Ludlow Music, 1963.

———. *Woody Guthrie: Roll On Columbia: The Columbia River Songs*, ed. Bill Murlin. Washington, DC: Department of Energy, 1988.

———. *Woody Guthrie Song Book*, ed. Harold Leventhal and Marjorie Guthrie. New York: Grosset and Dunlap, 1976.

———. *Woody Sez*, ed. Marjorie Guthrie, Harold Leventhal, Terry Sullivan, and Sheldon Patinkin. New York: Grosset and Dunlap, 1975.

Jackson, Mark Allan. *Prophet Singer: The Voice and Vision of Woody Guthrie*. Jackson: University Press of Mississippi, 2007.

Kaufman, Will. *Woody Guthrie, American Radical*. Chicago: University of Illinois Press, 2011.

Klein, Joe. *Woody Guthrie: A Life*. New York: Alfred A. Knopf, 1980.

Logsdon, Guy. "Woody Guthrie and His Oklahoma Hills." *Mid-America Folklore* 19 (Spring 1991): pp. 57–73.

———. "Woody Guthrie: A Biblio-Discography." In *Hard Travelin': The Life and Legacy of Woody Guthrie*, ed. Robert Santelli and Emily Davidson. Hanover, NH: University Press of New England for Wesleyan University Press, 1999, pp.181–243.

———. "Poet of the People." In Woody Guthrie, *Woody Sez*, ed. Marjorie Guthrie, Harold Leventhal, Terry Sullivan, and Sheldon Patinkin. New York: Grosset and Dunlap, 1975, pp. xi–xviii.

Lomax, Alan, Woody Guthrie, and Pete Seeger. *Hard Hitting Songs for Hard-Hit People*. Lincoln: University of Nebraska Press, 2012.

Longhi, Jim. *Woody, Cisco, and Me: With Woody Guthrie in the Merchant Marine*. Chicago: University of Illinois Press, 1997.

Partridge, Elizabeth. *This Land Was Made for You and Me: The Life and Songs of Woody Guthrie*. New York: Viking Books, 2002.

Partington, John S., ed. *The Life, Music, and Thought of Woody Guthrie*. Farnham, UK: Ashgate, 2011.

Santelli, Robert. *This Land Is Your Land: Woody Guthrie and the Journey of an American Song*. Philadelphia: Running Press, 2012.

Santelli, Robert, and Emily Davidson, eds. *Hard Travelin': The Life and Legacy of Woody Guthrie*. Hanover, NH: University Press of New England for Wesleyan University Press, 1999.

SELECTED DISCOGRAPHY

The Asch Recordings, 4 vols. Vol. 1, *This Land Is Your Land*; Vol. 2, *Muleskinner Blues*; Vol. 3, *Hard Travelin'*; Vol. 4, *Buffalo Skinners*. Smithsonian Folkways, 1999.

Ballads of Sacco and Vanzetti. Smithsonian Folkways, 1996.

The Columbia River Collection. Rounder Records, 1987.

Dust Bowl Ballads. Buddha Records, 2000.

Library of Congress Recordings. Rounder Records, 1988.

The Live Wire Woody Guthrie. Woody Guthrie Foundation, 2007.

Long Ways to Travel: The Unreleased Folkways Masters, 1944–1949. Smithsonian Folkways, 1994.

The Martins and the Coys. The Alan Lomax Collection. Rounder Records, 2000.

My Dusty Road. Rounder Records, 2007.

Nursery Days. Smithsonian Folkways, 1992.

Songs to Grow On for Mother and Child. Smithsonian Folkways, 1991.

Struggle. Smithsonian Folkways, 1990.

Woody at 100: The Woody Guthrie Centennial Collection. Smithsonian Folkways, 2012.

Woody Guthrie Sings Folk Songs. Smithsonian Folkways, 1989.

New Music from the Woody Guthrie Archives

Billy Bragg and Wilco. *Mermaid Avenue: The Complete Sessions*. Nonesuch Records, 2012.

Jonatha Brooke. *The Works*. Bad Dog Records, 2008.

Bob Childers, Jimmy LaFave, Joel Rafael, Slaid Cleaves, Eliza Gilkyson, Sarah Lee Guthrie and Johnny Irion, Ellis Paul, Kevin Welch, Michael Fracasso, *Ribbon of Highway, Endless Skyway*. Music Road Records. 2008.

Jay Farrar, Yim Yames, Anders Parker, and Will Johnson. *New Multitudes*, Rounder Records, 2012.

The Klezmatics. *Wonder Wheel and Happy Joyous Hanukkah*. Jewish Music Group, 2006.

Joel Rafael. *The Songs of Woody Guthrie*. Inside Recordings. 2009.

Rob Wasserman and various artists. *Note of Hope*. 429 Records, 2011

Wenzel. *Ticky Tock*. Contrar Musik, 2003.

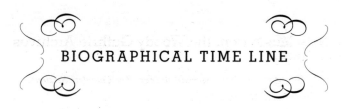

BIOGRAPHICAL TIME LINE

1878   Woody's father, Charley Guthrie, is born.

1888   Woody's mother, Nora Belle Sherman, is born.

1902   Charley Guthrie meets Nora Belle Sherman.

1904   NOVEMBER 24: Charley and Nora's first child, Clara Edna Guthrie, is born.

1906   DECEMBER 17: Charley and Nora's second child, Roy Guthrie, is born.

1907   The Guthrie family moves to Okemah, Oklahoma.

1912   Woodrow Wilson is nominated by the Democratic Party for president.

        JULY 14: Charley and Nora's third child, Woodrow Wilson Guthrie, is born.

1913   Woodrow Wilson is inaugurated as president of the United States.

The Guthrie family moves into the "Old London House" on South First Street, in Okemah.

1918   FEBRUARY: Charley and Nora's fourth child, George Guthrie, is born.

1919   MAY: Woody's older sister, Clara Edna Guthrie, dies in a fire.

1922   Oil is discovered in Cromwell, twelve miles southwest of Okemah.

MAY: Charley and Nora's fifth child, Mary Josephine Guthrie, is born.

1923   Okemah's population jumps to 15,000 because of the Cromwell oil.

1926   Charley sends two of his children, George and Mary Jo, to stay with his sister Maude in Pampa, Texas.

1927   Charley is severely burned in a fire. Nora Belle Guthrie is hospitalized. Charley moves to Pampa, Texas, to recuperate. Woody stays with Roy in Okemah, Oklahoma.

1927–1929   Woody lives with various families in Okemah.

1929   JUNE: Woody moves to Pampa, Texas.

1930   Woody forms his first band, the Corncob Trio, with his friends Matt Jennings and Cluster Baker.

JUNE 13: Nora Belle Guthrie dies at a hospital in Norman, Oklahoma.

1932   The Great Depression is at its worst.

1933   OCTOBER 28: Woody marries Mary Jennings. (They would divorce in 1943.)

1935   APRIL 14: Palm Sunday dust storms.

NOVEMBER: Woody and Mary's first child, Gwendolyn Gail Guthrie, is born.

1937   Woody leaves Pampa, Texas, and heads to California, the "Garden of Eden."

JULY: Woody and Mary's second child, Carolyn Sue Guthrie, is born.

SEPTEMBER: Woody and his singing partner Maxine "Lefty Lou" Crissman perform for the first time on KFVD radio.

DECEMBER: Woody, Mary, and their kids move to Glendale, California.

1938   JANUARY 22: Woody, Mary, and Allene Guthrie (Woody's cousin) and others travel to Tijuana, Mexico, to work on XELO radio. It doesn't work out, and they move back to California three weeks later.

JUNE 18: Woody and Maxine "Lefty Lou" Crissman end the *Woody & Lefty Show* on KFVD.

1939   MARCH: *The Grapes of Wrath* is published. It sells 420,565 copies in its first year and wins both the Pulitzer Prize and the National Book Award.

MAY 12: The first "Woody Sez" column appears in *The Daily Worker*.

JULY: Ed Robbins introduces Woody to Will Geer.

SEPTEMBER AND OCTOBER: Woody travels with Will Geer and others to support migrant workers organizing.

OCTOBER 7: Woody and Mary's third child, William Rogers Guthrie, is born.

1940   Woody and Mary appear as extras in Pare Lorentz's documentary *The Fight for Life*.

FEBRUARY: Woody moves to New York City and stays with the Geers.

FEBRUARY 18: Will Geer introduces Woody to Alan Lomax at a benefit concert for Spanish Loyalist refugees.

FEBRUARY 23: Woody writes "This Land Is Your Land" while living at the Hanover House in New York City.

MARCH 3: Pete Seeger for the first time hears Woody perform at a benefit concert for migrant workers hosted by the John Steinbeck Committee to Aid Agriculteral Organization.

MARCH 21, 22, 24: Woody records for Alan Lomax and the Library of Congress in Washington, D.C.

MAY: Woody records *Dust Bowl Ballads* for RCA Victor.

AUGUST: Woody appears on CBS radio in a pilot for a series called *Back Where I Come From*.

NOVEMBER: Woody appears on *Cavalcade of America* and is hired by the Columbia Broadcasting System.

1941 JANUARY: Leaves New York City to head across the country with Mary and their three children.

FEBRUARY: Woody gets a short-term job at KFVD in Los Angeles and begins work on the manuscript that will become *Bound for Glory*.

MARCH: Woody performs at an International Woman's Day Committee tea.

APRIL 3: Woody performs at an Okie benefit in Los Angeles.

APRIL 4: Woody performs at Barn Dance, a benefit for the Cannery and Agricultural Workers Union.

MAY 13: Woody begins his monthlong Columbia River project; he earns $266.66.

JULY: Upon returning to New York City, Woody joins up with the Almanac Singers on a trip west. They perform together in Detroit, Chicago, Milwaukee, Denver, and San Francisco.

JULY 7: Woody records *Deep Sea Chanties* and *Sod Buster Ballads* with the Almanac Singers.

AUGUST: Woody appears at Asheville, North Carolina, for a folk festival.

DECEMBER 7: Attack on Pearl Harbor.

DECEMBER 8: The United States enters World War II.

1942 JANUARY: Woody records home discs with the Almanacs in New York City and meets Marjorie Greenblatt Mazia at the Almanac House while rehearsing for *Folksay* (choreographed by Sophie Maslow).

JULY: RCA rejects Woody's proposal to record his war songs.

1943 FEBRUARY: Woody and Marjorie Guthrie's first child, Cathy Ann Guthrie, is born.

MARCH: *Bound for Glory* is published.

JUNE 5: Woody and his buddies Cisco Houston and Vincent "Jimmy" Longhi ship out with the Merchant Marine.

Woody, Marjorie, and Cathy move to 3520 Mermaid Avenue, Coney Island, in Brooklyn, New York.

1944 APRIL 16, 19, 20, 24, 25: Woody records for Moe Asch.

APRIL 19: Woody records fifty-seven songs with Cisco Houston.

OCTOBER: Woody performs in Chicago with the FDR Bandwagon.

Woody records *Struggle* for Asch Records.

1945 MARCH: Woody records for Moe Asch.

MARCH 10: With Ben Botkin, Herbert Haufrecht, Richard Dyer-Bennet, Charles Seeger, and Sonny Terry, Woody attends an all-day conference at Elizabeth Irwin High School on the place of folklore in a democracy.

MAY 8: Woody is inducted into the army.

NOVEMBER 13: Woody marries Marjorie Greenblatt Mazia. (They would divorce in 1953.)

DECEMBER 21: Woody is discharged from the army.

1946   *Songs to Grow On* is released.

Woody begins work on his unpublished novel *House of Earth*.

1947   Woody continues work on *House of Earth*.

FEBRUARY: Cathy Guthrie dies in an electrical fire.

JULY 10: Woody and Marjorie's second child, Arlo Guthrie, is born.

1948   JUNE TO NOVEMBER: Woody and Cisco Houston sing for Henry A. Wallace's presidential campaign.

DECEMBER 25: Woody and Marjorie's third child, Joady Guthrie, is born.

1950   JANUARY 2: Woody and Marjorie's fourth child, Nora Guthrie, is born.

FEBRUARY: Woody enrolls in Brooklyn College. He takes courses in philosophy, English, Spanish, and classical civilizations.

1952   Woody moves to Topanga Canyon, California, and meets Anneke Van Kirk.

1953   DECEMBER: Woody marries Anneke Van Kirk. (They would divorce in 1955.)

1954   Woody and Anneke have a daughter named Lorina Lynn.

Woody checks himself into Brooklyn State Hospital.

1956   Woody's father, Charley Guthrie, dies.

Woody is officially diagnosed with Huntington's disease.

MARCH 17: Benefit concert is held at Pythian Hall to raise money for Woody's children; this concert helps spark the folk revival.

MAY: Woody voluntarily checks out of Brooklyn State Hospital.

Woody is hospitalized at Greystone Hospital, New Jersey.

1959   Bob and Sidsel Gleason have Woody visit their home on Sundays for a hootenanny with friends.

1961   Bob Dylan visits Woody's home in Queens, New York, and is brought to visit Woody in the hospital.

Woody is transferred to Creedmore State Hospital.

1965   *Born to Win* is published.

1966   Woody receives the Conservation Service Award from the Department of the Interior.

1967   *Hard Hitting Songs for Hard-Hit People*, Woody Guthrie's songbook written with Alan Lomax and Pete Seeger in the 1940s, is published.

OCTOBER 3: Woody Guthrie dies at Creedmore State Hospital, Queens, New York.

1968   "Tribute to Woody Guthrie" concert is performed at Carnegie Hall.

1976   *Seeds of Man* is published.

1980   Joe Klein publishes *Woody Guthrie: A Life*, the first biography of Woody Guthrie.

1988   Woody Guthrie is posthumously inducted into the Rock and Roll Hall of Fame.

1996   The Woody Guthrie Archives opens in New York City.

1998   *Mermaid Avenue Volume 1*, an album of unpublished Guthrie lyrics set to music, is released by Billy Bragg and Wilco.

1999   The Smithsonian Institution Traveling Exhibition Service curates *This Land Is Your Land: The Life and Legacy of Woody Guthrie*. (The exhibit toured the United States through 2002.)

2000   FEBRUARY: Woody Guthrie posthumously receives the Lifetime Achievement Award from the National Academy of Recording Arts and Sciences (NARAS).

2012   JUNE: Woody Guthrie posthumously receives the inaugural Songwriters Hall of Fame Pioneer Award.

2012   JULY: Woody Guthrie's centennial. The *New York Times Book Review* announces the discovery of the completed *House of Earth*.

2013   FEBRUARY: *House of Earth* is published by Harper/Fourth Estate—Infinitum Nihil.